TIES THAT BIND

DEBBIE WHITE

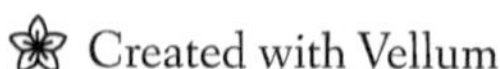 Created with Vellum

ACKNOWLEDGMENTS

Cover Design by Victorine Lieske

Editing done by Steve Mathisen

Debbie White Books
    Summerville, South Carolina

This book is dedicated to my husband. He not only stood by me while I cared for my mother, but he also helped me pick up the pieces after she was gone. He encouraged me to write this book, and I will always be thankful he was by my side.

QUOTE

Mid pleasures and palaces
Though we may roam,
Be it ever so humble,
There's no place like home.

~ John Howard Payne ~

PROLOGUE

I ALWAYS SAID my life began when I met Charles. He made everything better. We had a great life together, and despite my dysfunctional childhood, I'd say my life turned out pretty good. Sometimes, when I'd think back about all I'd been through, I'd shake my head in disbelief. It was hard for even me to believe some of the things I'd been through and discovered. It took me years to finally talk about it openly but once I did, closing those floodgates was next to impossible.

Those memories blazed brightly and were sometimes hard to put aside. So, I started keeping a journal in the hopes of writing my whole story someday. Like most people, time got away from me. I was thankful that Carole became interested in documenting my story.

Even though Charles was interested, there came a time when he felt it was water under the bridge and time to move forward. I told myself the same thing, but sometimes it's harder to do than you'd think.

When Carole said she'd like to write a book about my adoption and all the craziness involved, I was flattered. It was something we were doing together, and I enjoyed the closeness I felt when I shared my stories with her.

I knew there'd be a lot of information to cover, and it was hard sometimes to stay focused. Thankfully I had a great memory, and so I was able to give ages, and dates; which totally blew Carole's mind that I could remember so much. I looked forward to the afternoons she'd visit, and we'd discuss my story. My body might have been deteriorating, but my mind was like that of a twenty-year-old. I could remember even small details that surprised Carole.

I wasn't sure if I'd ever get to read the completed book, but even if I wasn't able to, I knew Carole would write it with all the sensitivity it required. I also knew she'd write it in my voice the best way she could. After all, it was my story, as Carole reminded me several times.

I didn't want anyone who read it to think I was angry about the things that happened to me. I'd forgiven them all. I had to. I couldn't carry that baggage around any longer. It doesn't mean I didn't still remember things. Carole would tell me I was like an elephant. I wouldn't forget anything. I could forgive, but forgetting; that was another thing.

IT WAS A BEAUTIFUL DAY, and although spring had not officially come it was pleasant enough to take a stroll around the grounds and visit the rose garden. Carole tenderly covered my legs with a lightweight cover and made sure I put on my sun visor. She packed a few essentials in my carry bag and strapped it to my wheelchair and off we went. I loved going outside, and Carole made sure I got out as much as possible. She pushed my wheelchair slowly avoiding the speed bumps in the parking area of my apartment building. She found the sidewalk and up and away we went. Soon we were rolling and talking. I don't know if I ever told her pointedly how much I enjoyed this, but I think she knew.

We ended up at the rose garden. It's where we usually went. It was there or the common area of the building so we could look at the tropical fish. It's funny, but back just a year or so I would have told you how boring that all sounded—visiting rose gardens and staring at tropical fish, but somehow it works when you're eighty-six and dependent on others.

I don't have any regrets, though. As difficult as life may have been, finding Charles more than made up for it, and the family we made was icing on the cake. My life was pretty ordinary once I met Charles. Well not really. Having your own private investigator's agency spiced things up considerably.

We worked as a team finding bad guys and the occasional unfaithful wife or husband—or runaway daughter. Life was fascinating and challenging in different ways, but we were doing it together.

What were the chances of me, with my background, getting a job at a private investigation firm, falling in love with the top investigator, and him helping me find out some of the answers to my questions? I'd say pretty slim, but that's just the way it happened.

For me to share my story, I have to start from the very beginning. As much as I tried to deny it, it shaped me. It made me who I am. And it starts right here.

IOWA DISTRICT COURT OF WOODBURY COUNTY

. . .

OFFICE of
COLLEEN LEE MOLSKOW 101 COURT
HOUSE
Clerk of District Court SIOUX CITY, IOWA

DEAR MRS. PHILLIPS:

We are unable to locate the birth record you have requested.

WE SUGGEST *that you write to the State Office:*

IOWA STATE DEPARTMENT OF HEALTH
Division of Vital Statistics
Des Moines, Iowa 50319

$4.00 EACH CERTIFICATE.
Yours Truly,
Clerk of District Court
Record Room

CHAPTER 1

I WAS SHAKING, tears streaming down my face. I'd had a nightmare. I didn't have many of them, but this one was a doozy. Carole took me by the hand, "Mom. I'm here. It looks like you've had a bad dream. What was it about?"

Wiping the tears from my face, I shrugged. "Irma."

"Irma?" She repeated.

I nodded.

Caroled hugged me for a long minute and then pulled away and locked eyes with me. "Do you mind if I write the details of your dream down? It might be pertinent later on for the book."

I nodded. "Of course, I'm delighted you've taken such an interest in writing my story. Although I don't know how many people will find it interesting," I said laughing.

Carole reached out and took my hand into hers. "It doesn't matter what anyone else thinks. I'm doing this for us." She leaned over and kissed me lightly on the cheek.

I had a lot to be thankful for. Despite a somewhat traumatic beginning, I can honestly say, my life was better for having endured all the difficult times of my childhood.

I often wondered if it was a mere coincidence I was drawn to Charles or was it part of some larger design. What are the odds of being adopted, moving to California, landing a job at a private investigation firm, and later marrying the best PI west of the Mississippi?

"I'm sorry dear, I struggled for so many years with not knowing who I was. It still haunts me from time to time." She nodded and smiled. "Your dad was so great about putting up with all the neurotic behavior about my past. I pretended, at first, that I didn't care. I did that for a long time. But gradually, it became all I could think about. He became determined to help me find answers," I said, a tear forming on my bottom lid.

"Mom—"

"Let me finish, dear. What I was going to say was you all are the most important thing in my life. Your dad would have been so proud of how you all have stepped up and taken care of your old Ma."

"Mom, we'd all do it again," she said leaning over and kissing me lightly on the forehead. "I still want to talk to you about all those years and write it all down. Let's get the complete story into book form that we can all keep and cherish as a memorial to how you persevered and triumphed over a bad start in life. But, for now, let's stop talking about it. Let's go look at the roses."

ADOPTION WAS DONE DIFFERENTLY BACK THEN. Babies were often adopted with a handshake, not the mounds of red tape that it takes nowadays. I guess I should be thankful that loving parents found me— although that description is a bit of a stretch.

My dad showed me love and kindness. Mom, on the other hand, was not very warm or kind, and occasionally could be physically abusive. She always seemed to be irritated with me.

When I was old enough to read, I was handed a newspaper clipping about my entry into the family. The clipping said I was found lying on a bed and was estimated to be about nine months old. I tried to visualize the look on their faces when they saw this bundle of unexpected joy. I also wondered how on earth a nine-month-old stayed still on a strange bed, in a strange house. It wasn't until years later that I found my first real clue that maybe Mother wasn't telling the whole truth.

I had a half-sister, Teresa, from my dads' first marriage—at least, that's what they said. She didn't like me all that much either. She was about sixteen years older than me, and for the longest time, I wondered if she could be my real mom, and the half-sister story was just a cover. The animosity she showed me intensified over the years.

My earliest memories were of my years in Iowa. My dad owned a pool hall, and on many nights, I'd find myself among the adults watching them shoot pool, playing cards and throwing back cold ones. I never thought anything of it. It was normal as far as I knew.

We were a lively bunch. On Friday nights, the family would get together in our pool hall and party the night away. I distinctly remember that many nights, when I was about four years old, I would walk out the back door, climb the steps to our apartment over the pool hall, and put myself to bed. Looking back, I don't think anyone missed me.

I had a couple of aunts and uncles who adored me.

They'd fuss over me and take me shopping, and we'd always end up at the ice-cream parlor. I always felt special when I was around them. If it weren't for them and my dad, life would have been pretty pathetic.

I had a couple of cousins, too. One, in particular, nicknamed Whitey, was more like an older brother. We rode bikes and played stickball in the street together along with the neighborhood kids.

It was during one of our playtimes that he spilled the beans about my real mother.

I ran home crying. Daddy was angry with Whitey for upsetting me.

Pulling him up by his suspenders, Daddy gave him a stern look. "Look here, Whitey. You don't know what you're talking about. Don't you ever say those ugly things to Patsy again," he said.

I still didn't know what the word meant, but I had a feeling that the word spewed from his mouth wasn't a good word.

When the Great Depression hit, we lost everything. The pool hall my dad just loved, the apartment overhead, and we would have lost the car too if it hadn't been for Daddy's sister. She saved the day by making all the late payments, with the stipulation we'd move to California.

My aunts and uncles had already made the trek

out to California, so we packed up the car with the few possessions we still had, and off to sunny California, we went.

THE GREAT DEPRESSION hit all the states, but California had a few programs that allowed the men to earn a little stipend by doing work for the CCC (California Conservation Corps). We moved into what would be considered the projects by today's standards. I started school—which I dearly loved, and we settled into California life easily.

Food was scarce. We received vouchers equivalent to food stamps to get certain foods such as cheese and bread. We were surrounded by acres of orchards of apples, peaches, and avocados. It was a natural food pantry right in our backyard. However, when fruit was the only choice to stop a growling stomach, you got tired of the taste and texture. I vowed that when I earned my own money, I'd buy cookies and cakes and never eat fruit again. Everyone in my family will tell you I have a sweet tooth. Just look in my dresser drawer, and you'll find bags of Hershey's Kisses.

Food wasn't the only thing that was scarce. Money was non-existent, but we had each other for company and entertainment. Whitey would sometimes bring over his guitar, and he and I would put on little skits and entertain the neighborhood, parents and all. I recall one such memory that involved singing a duet called Little Sir Echo. It was a popular song of the times, and to this day, I can recite the words.

After we had finished our performance, a few adults told us we should enter a local talent show that was being advertised.

I wasn't the least bit nervous performing on the stage in front of so many people. I was a natural, they said. It wasn't too much of a surprise that we'd won the grand prize - a plastic trophy, and a free ice-cream cone.

It was great to see Daddy, my aunts; Toots, Margie, and Annie in the audience. Mother was there too, but as usual, no smile, no reaction whatsoever. Thinking back, I don't think she even clapped for us.

Daddy rushed toward us, a broad smile plastered all over his face. Mother was by his side, but only a slight smirk emerged on hers. "You were so good. You should take your act on the road," he said.

I had a few friends, but my closest friend was Shirley. We met at school. She didn't live in the low-income apartments; her parents had a beautiful house in an excellent part of town. She would invite me over to play, and I was so in awe of her. She had her bedroom full of things that I could only dream of having. Her family was very kind to me, and I found myself not wanting to go home.

With her hands on her hips, Mother said in a disgusted voice, "You sure spend a lot of time over at Shirley's."

WE'D GIVEN up the severe winters of Iowa for sunny skies and warmer temperatures. It seemed like a good exchange. Life was hard, though, especially after Daddy got ill. I was just a young girl, but even then, the word cancer was scary. He tried to remain positive, even though our situation was anything but that.

I didn't realize just how sick he was until he was on his deathbed. Mother had the priest visit, and he performed last rites. Then the realization hit me and hit me hard. I ran out of the room crying. Life would never be the same. I knew that much.

Daddy died when I was about twelve. We didn't know a lot about cancer then. I just knew that one day he was fine, the next he was sick, and then he died. It happened so fast. At least, that's the way I remembered it. It was one of the saddest days of my life. I lost the only ally I had in the house.

When Daddy was alive, he acted as a buffer between mother and me. After he passed, my buffer was gone. Until I could stand up for myself, I would endure even more ponytail or arm yanking and a lot of yelling.

Mother drank occasionally, and it was after she'd had a few too many she made the revelation, "If only he'd kept his thing in his pants, you'd never been born." One could take this statement one of two ways, but she was letting me know she wasn't pleased being saddled with the outcome of Daddy's sexual exploits. I thought about that statement a lot, but it would be years before it meant anything concrete to me.

I kept to myself and planned my getaway. When I turned sixteen, I left home. It was the best thing I ever did. Living with Mother was too difficult. I reminded her of a part of her past she didn't want to remember. I didn't know what it was, but I could sense it within every fiber of me. She didn't even try to stop me. In fact, she held the door open for me as I left.

After I had left home, my half-sister Teresa and Mother moved back to Iowa. I was glad, as I didn't want to run into them. They'd made my life difficult enough. I wasn't stupid. After Daddy died, I could sense they felt I was more of a burden than a family member. I was happier without them in my life.

SHIRLEY'S FAMILY offered to let me live with them until I could save up enough money to live on my own. Shirley and I had plans to share a place together anyway, after graduation. Of course, plans don't always end as you hoped they would.

I knew that I needed to earn money, so I dropped out of high school and enrolled in secretarial school. Back then, you didn't have to have a high school diploma to enroll.

I learned how to type, take shorthand, and various other secretarial duties. I was ready for the workforce.

I held various jobs around the city where I used my newly learned skills. I was a good employee. I was prompt, courteous, and willing to learn new things.

Shirley and I had many fun and carefree days at the beach. Young and dumb, we both almost fell for a sailor or two. They were everywhere. Long Beach was a major port for the Navy.

Shirley and I had big dreams and settling down wasn't one of them–for that moment, anyway. So, after a few close calls with marriage proposals, Shirley and I decided it was time to leave her parent's house. Our first place was a small apartment over a mechanic's garage. It probably wasn't the smartest thing we'd ever done. Young men were constantly working on cars there. The wolf whistles and catcalls became more than a nuisance.

Shirley shot the grease monkeys a dirty look. "What are you looking at?" She said as she stormed up the steps to our apartment.

I saw it all from the window. Slamming it shut to let them know I didn't appreciate them upsetting my best friend, I waited for Shirley to enter the apartment. Seeing the look of disgust on her face, I offered a calming voice. "Those creeps don't mean any harm. They can't help themselves." I winked at her.

Shirley let out a sigh. "It may be time for us to look for a new place."

I started scouring the newspapers for something in a family-friendly environment.

"This sounds perfect, Shirley; a one bedroom flat near the beach."

"How much?" She asked as she pulled the paper out of my hands.

"Let's take a look at it. Maybe we can get second jobs to help pay for it?" I said reaching for the phone.

Those were the days. Shirley and I were like most

young women of that generation. We worked hard, but we also played hard. We could be found on many a Saturday night at the local club dancing the night away. And, because of our close proximity to Hollywood, Shirley and I would venture into town to see if we'd run into any famous stars... and we did. I recall seeing Clark Gable, and Rita Hayworth. Back then, stars were more humble, down to earth. They waved, spoke to us and then went about their business. We were thrilled, of course, as we were just nobodies trying to make it in the big, bad world.

Shirley and I stood holding each other. We trembled when she looked our way. I shrieked. "Oh. My. God. Look. It's Rita Hayworth."

Rita looked our way and then shot us the most beautiful smile. We both smiled back. She walked up to the roped off area we were standing behind, and gently took our autograph book out of our hands.

Shirley looked at me and hugged me. "Thank you, Miss Hayworth," we both said at the same time.

Like most young people, I struggled with paying the rent. I had no help from anyone in my family, but Shirley came from a well to do family, and she seemed to never be out of money.

I realized I needed a better job than the one I currently held at the local insurance company, and began my search. And that's how I landed the job at Phillips Private Investigation Firm and went to work for Charles Phillips. I needed the extra money to pay for that gorgeous flat, one block away from the beach.

It's funny how you remember things. Years later, we'd travel to the area where the gorgeous one bedroom flat was located. It was anything but. However, everyone who was someone wanted to live within walking distance to the beach. We were no different.

CHAPTER 2

I DISTINCTLY REMEMBER the day I interviewed for the job. Charles, the owner, asked the standard questions; how many words per minute I could type, if I could take shorthand, and what other skills I had. He then started to tell me a little bit about the job. I couldn't help but focus on his eyes. He had the prettiest blue-gray eyes I'd ever seen on a man.

In the beginning, I mostly answered the phone, made appointments, and looked after his calendar. I found his line of work interesting. He paid more than the job at the insurance company, which is what interested me first.

Women dressed in expensive clothing would come in and even through the closed door, I could hear them ranting and raving their suspicions about their husbands cheating on them. They would hire Charles to get to the bottom of it.

Of course, women weren't the only suspicious creatures who came through the doors. We had plenty of men come in and hire Charles to follow their wives around to see what they'd been up to all day while they were at work.

Soon, the Phillips PI firm was taking in new clients almost weekly, and Charles had a hard time keeping up. He'd been discussing hiring a helper when I had a bright idea. "Why can't I help?"

"You?"

"Yes, I find your line of work rather fascinating."

With his nose deep inside the files, he said, "Who are we going to get to do the clerical work?"

"That would be easy. I can place an ad at the secretarial school. There are plenty of young ladies who'd be interested." I said eagerly.

He kept looking for a file, and sort of ignored me. I didn't want to say any more but felt I was the best person for the job. I had a very inquisitive nature, and the work interested me. I walked back around to my desk and was just about to sit down when Charles pulled out the file he was looking for and slammed the drawer shut. As he walked back into his office, file in hand he looked over his shoulder. "Place the ad. We'll go from there."

I typed up the ad on a three by five card. Yelling into the office that I'd be back, I turned the sign on the door that said 'OUT TO LUNCH' and walked the three blocks to the school.

It wasn't long after placing the ad that Ms. Kelly Parker interviewed for the job. She was attractive with delicate features, petite in size, and long, flowing blonde hair. Her eyes were vivid blue with enough mascara for three women. She wore a smart looking two-piece blue suit trimmed in white with matching blue pumps. She carried a white purse, and her cologne had a familiar smell, which later I'd learned was Chanel Number 5.

I asked her the standard questions: how many words per minute could she type, and what other skills she had. I was satisfied she'd be perfect for the job. I called Charles in to meet her and see if he had anything more to ask or add. He walked in, looked her up and down, and then being a man of few words said, "When can you start?"

It took a few days to get Ms. Parker familiar enough with things before I left her in her new position. She appeared to be very comfortable. Charles and I both felt she was a good fit for the firm, and later, we'd agree she wasn't too bad on the eyes either.

I BEGAN WORKING CLOSELY with Charles on several of his cases. It was easy to blend in and follow the women we were hired to watch. They just saw me as another woman out shopping or having lunch. Little did they know, I reported my findings back to Charles, and sometimes they were pretty revealing. I witnessed women being kissed and hugged, checking into motels in the middle of the day, and all sorts of suspicious behavior. I loved the excitement my new job provided, and I didn't feel the least bit guilty spying on people.

Shirley was used to me coming home with outrageous stories. She always seemed to be interested. Sitting across from me with her legs crossed, she gave me her full attention. "I can't believe they didn't even notice you were spying. You must be good," she said nodding her head.

I leaned in, excited to give her more details. "I was looking over the menu, trying to eavesdrop and not be suspicious. It's really exciting," I told her.

One of the scariest jobs we did was for a millionaire who wanted to see what his trust fund daughter was up to. He could have chosen any private investigator within a fifty-mile radius, but he chose us. He wanted to remain low-key and decided we would provide the cover he needed.

We met with Mr. Solomon, and he laid out the scenario. Apparently, his daughter had become very secretive regarding her whereabouts. She was twenty years old and within two weeks of her twenty-first birthday. On that occasion, she would begin receiving an allowance of twenty-five thousand dollars a week. That would persist until the age of twenty-five when that amount would be bumped up to thirty thousand. He wanted assurances that she wasn't hanging around bad people. He had a hunch she might be.

Charles brushed his hand across his mouth, and his hand ended up in his lap. He crossed his legs. Then he uncrossed them. "This could either be an easy case or a very difficult one. It seems there may be more to the story than meets the eye."

I nodded I understood. Eager to learn, I leaned in and said, "Just tell me what you want me to do."

CHAPTER 3

MR. SOLOMON HAD GIVEN us a detailed itinerary of his daughter's typical day. Charles and I set out to see what we could find. The first couple of days we didn't discover anything significant. On the first day, she went to a bakery; ordered a sticky bun and coffee, and ate it at a little bistro table outside—alone. Later, she went to the library, browsed the stacks, and left empty-handed. She then returned home.

The next day, she went to the department store and tried on eight dresses before leaving empty-handed. To Charles and me, this didn't seem to be a young woman going through her money like water. She didn't even spend any now, leaving us wondering if her father's fears were unfounded.

Charles paced the office floor. "Something just

doesn't add up. This gal is either very slick or innocent."

I watched him as he pondered. He looked out the window and then whirled around. "What do you think? You're a woman."

Startled by his question, I paused before answering. I smoothed out my skirt. "I think she's hiding something."

After following her for over a week, we were about to report back to Mr. Solomon that we hadn't uncovered anything that would make us suspect she wouldn't handle her inheritance wisely. But then we discovered something so surprising, I had a hard time believing it (even though I'd already voiced my opinion that she was up to something). Charles, on the other hand, said he'd seen it all and wasn't shocked by her behavior. Looking back, I shouldn't have been too shocked either as my own daddy did a little gambling.

Apparently, Ms. Solomon was running numbers for a notorious bookie. She was meeting the clients at the bakery, library, department store and the final place we caught her in the act—at a nursing home while visiting her grandmother.

We'd been told by her father that her grandmother —his mom lived there. We saw her go into the nursing home and waited in the car for almost an hour before she came back out. We didn't suspect any funny business but wanted to stay on her trail.

I noticed him first. Some guy with jet-black hair slicked back with enough grease to fry a chicken. I saw her slip him a large envelope and alerted Charles.

We watched as he stuck it down his pants. She quietly walked away one direction, and he went the other. We kept an eye on him but waited until she got in her car and drove away before we proceeded to follow ol' slick. Sure enough, he led us to a local pool hall infamous for gambling. We decided to watch her a bit more carefully, now that we had an idea of what might be going on. That's when things got interesting.

Each day, she went to different places, trying to throw us off the scent, but by the end of the day, she always led us to some individual that was on the receiving end of money. We weren't sure yet, but we were pretty sure money was in the envelopes she turned over.

"We need to find out who is giving her the envelopes to deliver," Charles said.

Nodding my head, I exclaimed, "I agree."

We continued our surveillance, and before long, we discovered Ms. Solomon was involved with one of the biggest gambling families west of the Mississippi River. Mr. Las Vegas, as he was affectionately called, had a reputation for being pretty mobster like, and I was getting a bit scared.

"Charles, maybe we've met our match. This guy is bad news."

"We're not going to confront him; we're just gathering evidence for Mr. Solomon."

"I know, but, I'm still nervous. What if he puts a hit out on us?"

"We're not going to get that close. We just need a bit more proof."

The danger we were exposed to was still nerve-racking. This guy meant business. If he thought for a second, we were about to interfere with his business, or get the police involved, Charles and I would have been wearing cement shoes.

Lucky for us, Charles was right, and we got the evidence we needed to report back to the client. He was saddened by the news and wasn't sure how he was going to handle it. That wasn't for us to decide, or to know. We just wanted payment for finding out what his daughter was up to and go on our merry way. He handsomely rewarded us, and we never heard from him or his daughter again.

"You know, we make a great team," Charles said lightly touching my hand.

I stared into his blue-gray eyes, and my heart started beating a mile a minute.

I HAD ALWAYS FELT comfortable with him—even from the very first moment we met. Now, I felt something else. I knew it probably wasn't wise to get involved with my employer. We were working together day in and day out, and it was natural to form a bond. But what I was beginning to feel was more than that. I wondered if he felt the same.

We began spending a lot of time together—not just working cases in the office or out in the field, but after-hours as well. Most of the time, work was the underlying reason for our after-hours visits. However, I found myself laughing at his jokes, watching his every move and hanging on to his every word as if it were his last. We'd order Chinese take-out, pepperoni pizzas, or giant sub sandwiches and devour our meals over a coffee table spread with pads of paper—that contained our notes for one of our current cases. I loved being with him.

Over the course of our courtship, I found out Charles had ended up in California when he was in the Air Force. He liked it so well he decided to stay and make California his home. His mom, dad, and an older brother lived in Michigan. His sister, Carole had been tragically killed by a hit and run truck driver when she was only five.

He was five years older, and because he'd traveled the world and learned about different cultures. He seemed more worldly than I was and I was fascinated by his stories.

While he was in the military, Charles had traveled to Guam, and Japan, and saw how other cultures lived. We both liked the idea and looked forward to the day we could travel. His investigative firm was growing by leaps and bounds; it was a real possibility that his dream would come true.

WE BOTH LOVED ANIMALS TOO, so when we got an opportunity to try and find the missing pug we dug in our heels and tried to locate the missing pup–after our initial outburst of laughter, that is.

The pug we were looking for was approximately three years old, and the woman who lost him was devastated. The way she spoke about "Henry" had you believing she was talking about her son. Her relationship with the dog was extreme, but nevertheless, real for her. We promised to do our best and find Henry.

Charles and I started our search by looking at all the area parks.

"That would be the first place on my list if I were a dog," I told Charles.

He nodded. He held the black and white photo of Henry the lady had given us, and we headed out to the first of many parks to see if we could find him. Our primary concern, as well as Mrs. Peters, was Henry's safety.

We parked the car at one of the downtown parks. It was a Saturday and children, parents and dogs filled the park with laughter–and yes, barking dogs. It was a hectic day at the park, and I was a bit overwhelmed trying to stay focused on all the four-legged friends.

"Over here," I called to Charles.

"Nope. That's not a pug," Charles said, shaking his head.

I continued walking among the smiling faces in search of old Henry. Well, he wasn't very old, but it made Charles and I laugh thinking about the candy bar and the dog we were looking for.

After a full day of searching parks, Charles and I headed home feeling a bit defeated.

"How hard is it to find a small cream-colored dog with a smashed-up face?"

I shrugged my shoulders. "Beats me. I thought for sure we'd find him at one of these parks," I said.

"What's our plan of action for tomorrow?" I asked.

"We'll check the pound. Maybe someone turned him in," Charles said.

"The pound! We should have checked there first," I said feeling a bit foolish I hadn't thought of that.

"The park was a good idea. As friendly a dog as Henry is, coupled with the fact that he loves children, made it a great place to start."

I nodded. "I hate the thought of Henry sleeping in a cage."

Charles reached over and lightly rubbed my leg. It gave me goosebumps when he did that. Something about his touch always did that to me.

The following day we went to the two local shelters to see if Henry was there. To our surprise, he was not.

"I'm perplexed for sure. He wasn't at the parks. He wasn't at the pound. Where in the heck could he be?" Charles said.

"I think we should contact Mrs. Peters. She may have some additional information," I said.

"I think that's a brilliant idea, Pat."

We met with Mrs. Peters as Charles suggested. In the course of our conversation with her, she let it be known that she was in the middle of a divorce.

"Mrs. Peters, is there any way that Mr. Peters could have taken Henry?"

Mrs. Peters lowered her head. She fidgeted with the buttons on her sweater. "I didn't want to think he would. But the truth is, he was always jealous of little Henry," she said blinking back tears.

Charles looked over at me. I shrugged my shoulders.

I stood up and walked over to the desk. I took a pad of paper and pen and handed it to Mrs. Peters. "Please write his address down."

"You wait in the car. I don't expect any trouble, but just in case," Charles said.

I nodded. This was one of the strangest cases we'd been on.

I could see Charles on the stoop talking to a woman. She had long blonde hair and appeared to be trim. She was using her hands and once put them firmly on her hips. The body language told me she was agitated that Charles was questioning her. I was about to exit the car when Charles turned around and with head hanging down walked toward the car.

"That's the new girlfriend. She said he's at work, and she doesn't know anything about Henry. She was a bit upset that we visited their house today."

"That's too bad. We have a job to do," I said matter of fact.

Charles shot me a quick grin. "Wow. You're a bit tough today," he said squeezing my leg.

"I'm learning from the best," I whispered.

Charles started the car. We were just about to drive off when the woman from the house came running out and in her arms–Henry!

I threw open the car door and stood on the sidewalk.

"You. You had him all the time?"

She handed him over to me.

"Take him. I didn't want to have him. He made me do it."

Charles approached the woman. "What do you mean, he made you do it?"

"He said Henry was valuable. He wanted to use him as a negotiating tool. Mrs. Peters was to get a hefty sum of money in the divorce proceedings."

Now I'd heard everything. Holding a harmless little pup as a negotiating tool in a divorce proceeding.

I shook my head. "I'm just glad he's safe. We'll return him to Mrs. Peters," I said.

I slid in the front seat of the car holding Henry on my lap. He licked my face, and it made me giggle. He was such a cute little guy with his smashed up little face. I petted him and tried to comfort him while Charles finished up with the girlfriend. I never did get her name. We called her Blondie.

"She's going to have to explain to Mr. Peters why she gave up Henry. I don't envy her. Sounds like he's an idiot. I wonder what she saw in him," Charles said.

I blinked a couple of times. Charles did not see the forest for the trees. "She went along with it for the money, Charles."

He nodded. "It always comes down to the money, doesn't it?"

I softened my smile and gazed lovingly into his eyes. "It will never come down to money with us."

CHAPTER 4

CONSIDERING how my life had begun, I was elated to see how it had evolved. I was a pretty happy person. Oh sure, I had my days of self-doubt, and mild depression but Charles seemed to bring out only the best in me, and I didn't think about the bad days very often.

I wrote to the city records department to get a certified copy of my birth certificate only to be told there wasn't one. Instead, I received a copy of a certificate of live birth with both my adoptive parents listed, Irma and Lyle. I wrote again, inquiring about the adoption specifically, and received a letter saying the adoption was closed, and no information could be released. It seemed one roadblock after another was being placed in my way as I tried to discover who my biological parents were.

As Charles and I got to know one another, my adoption became a topic of interest for him. His investigative personality was intrigued by it, and he would often ask me questions about it. I'd try to tell him as much as I could recall, but much of it was fuzzy. I told him I thought I was connected to the family in some way, and that some big secret was being kept buried. I shared with him the few words I could recall that had slipped from family member's mouths, and how my daddy's sisters—my aunts loved me to pieces. The biggest clue that I may belong to the family in some way was the way in which Irma; my mother, and my half-sister, Teresa treated me.

As I aged, I felt less threatened by that situation, and, although I was still interested in knowing my past, it wasn't much more than a curiosity. The driving need to know would not come until years later.

It was after one of our big deep discussions involving Iowa and my adoption that he leaned in and kissed me. I wasn't expecting it but welcomed it just the same. His lips were warm as he gently pushed my lips apart. I don't recall much about that evening, my head swirling from warm, wet kisses. But that night changed our relationship forever, and Charles became the family I'd never had.

In between finding lost spouses and the occasional

runaway teenager, we nourished our relationship. Soft kisses turned into longer, more romantic kisses, and the passion I felt deep in the pit of my stomach let me know Charles was the one.

WE DECIDED we'd be married by the Justice of the Peace—a simple ceremony for simple people. I invited my aunts; Toots and Margie to witness the ceremony and celebrate the marriage. We went to dinner at a nice restaurant and decided our future over steak and lobster.

We were doing pretty well financially, so Charles said we could take a few days and go on a honeymoon.

I'd never flown before and was a little scared when he suggested Hawaii. Nevertheless, the explorer in me took over, and I was excited about my first flight over the ocean to the sandy shores of Hawaii.

We stayed in an ocean view room, drank funny little fruity drinks with umbrellas, and took long walks along the beach holding each other tight. We truly were in paradise.

Not knowing the extent of Charles's experience in the sex department, and not wanting to know either, I was a little nervous about our first night together as husband and wife. Needless to say, we found our niche.

AFTER WE HAD RETURNED to the mainland, we settled into marriage great. Our union was a happy one filled with much laughter and kindness. I craved those things, and Charles made sure every day was filled with both.

We still were hitting the pavement, chasing bad guys, or gals, and reaping the monetary awards for a job well done. The work seemed to never end. We were newlyweds, though, and so in between our jobs, we always made time for one another.

I'D NEVER FELT any love for Irma or Teresa—definitely not the way I felt love for Charles. However, when my aunt brought over the obituary notice for Irma, I did feel a little pang, deep in the pit of my stomach. I guess because that part of the puzzle was now gone from my life forever.

"Who sent this to you?" I asked my aunts.

Straightforward, just like I like it, Aunt Margie said, "Teresa."

Running my finger over the glossy bookmarked obituary, I nodded and asked, "Where's she at these days?"

"Still in Sioux City," Aunt Toots replied.

"Ah, yes, I see that now," I said, feeling a bit stupid that I'd asked the question in the first place.

"Well, thanks for this," I said holding up the clipping.

Aunt Annie said, "I know you haven't had any contact with the family back there—"

"Nope, and I don't plan to," I said directly to all three of them.

"Just think about it, honey. You just might want them in your life one of these days," Aunt Margie murmured.

Being the strong-willed character that I was, I replied, "No way. They were never there for me, why would I ever need them? You're all the family I ever need," I said looking first at Margie, and then Annie before settling my eyes on Toots.

"Well, that brings us to another topic. Whitey is going to drink himself to death." Aunt Toots bellowed.

"It's a real shame too because he just got a record contract with RCA," Aunt Margie said before adding under her breath, "What an idiot."

"I'll talk to him. I'm kind of busy helping Charles with the business, but I'll make time to see him."

I DID as I promised and tried to talk some sense into Whitey, but drinking and women seemed to be his passion these days along with singing and making records. It was a shame that was the path he chose.

I got him alone. I gently touched him on the arm. I wanted him to know I cared. "Whitey everyone is concerned you're going to end up hurting yourself, or worse, someone else. Can't you slow down on the drinking?" I pleaded.

I learned a long time ago that you can't help those who will not help themselves. Whitey went on to become a famous singer and guitar player, but his drinking made him a one-hit wonder, and sadly, it eventually cost him his life. What a shame too. He had talent.

With Charles, life was better than perfect. Or so it should have been. He was a wonderful husband, a great provider, and he was the love of my life. So why did I feel like I was missing something?

Charles thought maybe once we started our family, the emptiness I felt, would be filled with the laughter of children. I hoped he was right.

The pitter-patter of little feet was exactly what I needed, and our first child, a boy, we named Charles Jr. filled me up with more joy than I thought was possible.

Charlie, as we affectionately called him, was the love of our lives. We worshiped him as much as any parents could. He was happy, healthy, and we were madly in love with that little boy.

I still helped with the business, but mainly just paperwork. I wanted to be a stay at home mom for Charlie. That was my priority. Now and then, I would get sad about Charlie not having grandparents nearby. But, having my aunts nearby was the next best thing, and they smothered him in love just like they'd done with me as a small child.

Charles leaned around and kissed me on the cheek. "Everything ok?" He must have seen the tears in my eyes.

I shrugged my shoulders. "I wish Charlie had family nearby."

Charles cocked his head, "family?"

"Grandparents," I said.

He nodded. "Pat, Charlie is not the only kid without grandparents," he said walking toward the fridge.

I reached into the drawer and handed him the bottle opener.

Popping the top off his beer, I watched him take a swish of the cold brew. "He'll be well-rounded and well-loved," he said patting me on the behind.

When Charlie was about two, along came Carole. Carole was named after Charles's little sister who'd been killed. Our Carole was a quiet child, but she filled our hearts as much as Charlie did.

It was wonderful having the kids only two years apart. To this day, they're close. We had a little longer break in between Carole and child number three. We decided to change letters and capture names that started with "P" like my own, Patricia.

Peter was a delightful child, but headstrong. He was always challenging my authority and kept Charles and me on our toes. He would be the child that continually pushed the boundaries.

There was about eight years difference between Peter and Carole, but she didn't see him as a bothersome little brother. She loved to take him for walks and play with him outside. Charlie was also a big help with his little brother. I always knew that if Peter were with either of the older children, he'd be well taken care of.

Life couldn't have been any better. I had a house with a picket fence on a tree-lined street, married to the love of my life, and three beautiful children. What more could a girl want?

I asked myself that question over and over on the days when I couldn't get out of bed, or on the days when the children irritated me, or the days I'd pick an argument with Charles or the children.

I tried to take Charles approach that some things we just can't change. I guess I was a fixer and didn't realize it. I knew too many years had passed for any sort of reconciliation with Irma, or Teresa, or any of my long-lost family. Yet, sometimes I found myself wanting to scream at the top of my lungs that I wanted answers, and I wanted them now.

My life probably wasn't much different than many others who were brought up in a dysfunctional family.

Some children can rise above their circumstances and put all the ugliness behind them. I tried. Charles made it easy to move forward, and after the children came along, I found even more purpose for my life.

But, I wasn't prepared for losing the few remaining family relatives. I would say blood relatives, but I wasn't sure of that. However, my aunts were the closest thing I had, and when one by one they passed away, I felt a little of me go with them. I was particularly saddened by the death of my Aunt Margie.

Charles and I had moved, leaving my aunts in Southern California. Now, distance separated us. As our children grew, they didn't seem to miss having aunts, uncles or even grandparents around, something I had wanted for them when they were younger. It would not be until years later during one of my talks with Carole that I would learn she missed not having extended family around.

After the children were grown and gone, I would make an occasional bus trip to Southern California. I'd try to find out some details about my adoption in more subtle ways. After a while, I gave up. My aunts were not interested in dredging up old stuff, and I tried to feel the same way.

My last visit with Aunt Margie only seemed to

highlight the fact that Aunt Toots and Aunt Annie were already gone.

I told myself that I wouldn't ask her. But it was hard to see her slipping away along with, perhaps, my last best chance of knowing the truth.

CHAPTER 5

ON AUNT MARGIE'S DEATHBED, I asked her if she knew who my real parents were. I felt like it was my last opportunity, and I went for it.

I took her hand in mine. Her hand felt cold, and I could feel the frailty, bone by bone. Her eyes were closed, but she was conscious. "Aunt Margie. Is there anything you want to tell me about my daddy?"

She squeezed her eyes tighter. I wasn't sure if she was in pain or trying to gather her thoughts. "Patsy, let it go."

I nodded even though she couldn't see it. She was going to take the big secret to her grave.

She opened her eyes and turned her head toward me. "There's a black box in the bureau. It's yours. Take it. Maybe it will give you some comfort." With that, she closed her eyes. She was gone.

I retrieved the black metal box and remembered seeing it in our home when I was little. It was crudely made (my daddy had made it out of some type of tin), but it had a latch, a handle, and was fireproof.

Inside, it held two copies of the article that ran in the local Sioux City paper regarding me, a glossy bookmark style obituary of Irma, and the obituary from my dad. Also, in the box were some trinkets; a ring that appeared to be homemade, dog tags, and my dad's social security card.

There were a few picture albums as well. I opened each one, and the story of me, and my family began to unfold; starting in Iowa and ending in California.

Later, I was sitting alone in the living room. The children were in school, and Charles was at the office. I retrieved the old black box from our closet and held Daddy's dog tags in my hands. I placed the metal ring on my finger. It was too big; probably made for a man or a woman with a fat finger, maybe Irma, I wondered, or perhaps Teresa's mother.

It was during quiet times like this that my mind

wandered, and I began to recall times in Iowa like the time when Daddy was arrested for making moonshine.

It was common knowledge that Daddy made the best. He'd barter other goods and money in exchange for the alcohol. Mother even got into making it.

I recall hearing that someone had stiffed Daddy on a payment of one form or another. An argument ensued, and in the end, someone must have ratted on Daddy because the cops showed up at our house.

I was so young, I didn't realize what he was doing was illegal. When the cops showed up, I could just hear bits and pieces for the reason of their visit.

I guess I thought I was helping Daddy because when they brought me in and asked me what I knew, I showed the cops right where the stuff was hidden. My mother's eyes grew wide as she watched me lift up the loose floorboard and point to what was below.

Then they hauled Daddy off to jail.

I was crying and couldn't understand what I'd done. Mother with her hands on her hips furrowed her brow. "Now look what you've done," she said shaking her finger at me.

Mother kept her stash hidden in the wringer washer, suds and all. Years later, I'd play the scenario over, but instead of showing the cops the loose floorboard, I took them to the wringer washer.

Daddy wasn't angry at me in the least, though. He knew I didn't mean to get him in trouble. I was just an innocent child thinking I was helping out.

After he'd been at the jail for a few hours, I pleaded with Mother to take me to visit him.

She let out an over exaggerated sigh. She turned her back as if to ignore me. I tugged on her dress. "I want to see Daddy," I pleaded.

Suds were flying as she tried to wash dishes. My crying became louder and began to be more like wailing. Finally, she tossed the dishrag into the sink and grabbed me by the arm. "Let's go," she roared.

I smiled even though she was pulling me along by the arm. I was going to see my daddy.

Daddy, happy to see me, smiled showing all of his missing teeth. We visited for a while. When the guards told him it was dinnertime. Daddy quietly asked them if I could stay and eat with him.

Mother huffed and puffed about what an idiotic idea it was. "You're going to let a child stay here and eat dinner with you?" She bellowed.

He nodded his head. He was a man of few words.

It was one of the best dinners I'd had in a long time - Spaghetti and meatballs.

I also recalled another time when Daddy had drunk too much of his moonshine; Mother made him sleep out in the car. I begged and pleaded with her to let him come inside, but that only made it worse for the both of us. She tried hard to break up our little partnership, but it didn't work. I loved him dearly, and the day he died, I lost the one and only real parent I knew loved me the way I loved them.

Once in a while, Daddy would sit on the front porch and sing to me. Sometimes, my cousin, Whitey would play his guitar.

Mother would come out, look at us with a stern face letting us know we were too loud. "Lyle, it's getting late. The neighbors are going to complain," she said.

When we'd ignore her, and she'd walk back inside letting the screen door slam as if to tell us we were bothering her. We didn't stop. In fact, we sang even louder, and Whitey strummed his guitar with more force. We loved getting under her skin. If she'd only known what we said about her behind her back, she'd have been furious.

Tears would often form in my eyes when I had these flashbacks. I tried to be strong in front of Charles and the children, but for better or worse, memories of the past had me wanting to pursue the truth about my parents or, at least, the truth surrounding my birth.

The memories of my days in Iowa pulled me back there, like it or not.

I SPENT hours writing to various agencies in search of any details regarding my birth or adoption. It was a slow, painstaking process, but information began filtering in

I was also able to locate some census reports, and they gave me the most clues. I found dates that I could work with, and those allowed me to find entries that listed my mother, Irma as a child. It was another path to search. That date would have put her around sixteen to eighteen years old. It showed the address as a convent in Sioux City. That piqued my interest.

I vaguely remembered hearing that she had wanted to be a nun and that she married Daddy instead. I also recalled pictures of crosses, churches, and bibles placed on shelves, which seemed hypocritical to the non-Christian way she treated my daddy and me.

I didn't believe for a second that she was ever a nun, or that she even joined the convent to be one. I thought all along it was just a ruse to cover up her un-Christian ways, and better yet, give her an alibi for her whereabouts during the early years. Everything was a mystery about that woman. How the heck did she ever get her claws into Daddy? I wondered about that more than anything else.

I RECALL the day I told the kids I was adopted. It wasn't planned, it just presented itself. Carole and I had had a particularly stressful day.

It was like any other morning, with the kids getting ready for school. Carole was taking too long like any typical teenager. Looking back, I wondered if she actually was taking too long, or I was just impatient. I called up to her from downstairs telling her she needed to get a move on. I had prepared breakfast, and it was getting cold. She didn't respond to my yelling, so I tried once again. Still, there was no response. I stormed up the stairs to find her mimicking me in her mirror, and the anger overcame me. I don't even remember doing it. I reached out and slapped her across the face. She turned to me, touching the red, warm spot from my slap.

"I hate you. You're crazy." Carole yelled as she ran down the stairs.

"Don't forget your lunch," I called out as if nothing had happened.

I stood in the doorway of her room for a moment, my breathing labored, and my heart beating a mile a minute. What had I just done?

All of a sudden, a distant memory came flooding into my mind. My own mother had done similar things to me when I was much younger than Carole.

When the kids came home from school, they walked into a house filled with the smell of warm chocolate chip cookies just out of the oven. This is how I would ask for forgiveness. I guess it worked. No one made mention of my hysterical outburst or unacceptable behavior regarding this instance, or any other.

Later that evening, over a dinner of favorites, Charles and I told the kids about me. Peter was not particularly moved by the discussion. But Carole and Charlie were all ears, especially Carole.

"That's kind of cool, Mom. You may have brothers and sisters you didn't even know about," Carole boasted.

"I don't know about that, Carole. I do have a sister. Her name is Teresa," I said not wanting to share that part.

"Aunt Teresa," Carole remarked.

I nodded. "Listen. It's not going to be anything glorious here. We're not going to reunite with lost family and pick up where we left off," I explained.

"Mom, you don't know how it will turn out. It's been so long," Carole said.

"I can tell you there is no love lost here, guys. That's the truth. I'm just telling you about my adoption and my life before California, in case anything comes up about it," I said matter-of-factly.

I also told them the story of dropping out of school and enrolling in secretarial school. I was nervous about their reaction, but the reality was, I was the one who'd help the kids with most of their homework, especially spelling and English. Charles would assist them with their Math. He was good with numbers.

I was self-taught in many areas, which made the fact I only had an eighth-grade education easier to hide. I loved to read, and I tried to learn as much as I could on many subjects. Charles never thought any less of me for not having a high school education. Even so, I knew it was the one thing my children would get. I'd see to it.

The children just stared at me. Charlie Jr. took it all in stride, I suppose. Carole was trying to make sense of it all, and Peter...well, Peter couldn't have cared less. He was too young. His concentration was on baseball and football.

As Carole became a young woman, she and I would have deep discussions about it. She never held it over my head; she'd just say every now and then, "Secrets aren't good. It's not a healthy way to develop and foster relationships." I could hear the sincerity in her voice. I vowed to her, no more secrets.

I felt such a big relief. A weight had been lifted, and I could begin to heal. Now that I'd included the kids, they were a little more curious and occasionally would ask me what I'd found out if they saw me looking over documents I'd received in the mail. I created a binder to keep everything organized. Carole helped me by putting them in a protective sleeve, and as she placed them in the binder, she would read aloud what they said.

"Mom, why does it say Irma was an inmate at the convent?"

"I believe that's the terminology they used back then when an orphan lived there. I'm not sure, though. I guess it's one of the mysteries, huh?" I said, loving that she was interested in my journey.

CHAPTER 6

SHORTLY AFTER THIS REVELATORY MEETING, Charles said to me in his always calming voice, "Pat... Carole came to me. She's worried about you." I lowered my head in shame.

"I didn't mean to slap her. It just happened," I said in between sobs.

"I know you'd never hurt any of the kids," he said hugging me softly.

"I think it's time you talked to someone. I don't care who, but a professional," he said with a little more tone than he would typically use with me.

I realized he was right. I loved my family so much. I had to break this ugly chain of lashing out for no apparent reason. I needed professional help. I couldn't let my adoption, or the hatred I felt for the only mother

I'd ever known ruin my relationship with my children or my husband.

I began seeing a psychiatrist. We'd meet once a week and just talk. Over time, she was instrumental in helping me let go of the hatred. She reminded me that many people suffered worse situations than I had. She also reminded me that we are all in control of our destiny and that we can't hold others responsible for the outcome. She was right. It was what Charles and I had taught our children.

"I understand what you're saying. I believe it to be true," I concluded to the doctor during one of our visits.

"Believing is half the battle," she said calmly.

"How do I keep the bad thoughts from creeping back in?" I asked.

"That's the hard part, Pat. Not everyone is happy every second of the day. We have periods of sadness, and even to some extent, depression. You can't let it rule your life. You have a lot to be thankful for."

"Oh yes, I sure do," I said smiling thinking of my little family.

"What you must do, if you can, is put it behind you. This doesn't mean you forget. It's part of who you are. You shouldn't dismiss that. However, you've heard the saying, when you are given nothing but lemons, make lemonade," I nodded I had.

After a number of sessions, I was feeling much more positive about my situation and felt that it was time to address the issue head on.

"I've been thinking about visiting Sioux City," I said.

Nodding her head, she replied, "That might be helpful."

"I haven't mentioned anything to Charles about it. It would be after the kids are older. It's just a thought I had. Maybe if I could get some answers, I could finally put it to rest."

"I think it's an idea worth considering. You and Charles can make that decision."

I was content with our meetings, and Charles said he saw a lighter side of me. He thought it was working.

Our family was like most others. We had trials and tribulations, fears, and anger moments. We tried hard to move past all the things life threw at us, and for the most part, I'd say we were successful.

Eventually, all the kids graduated from high school. Charlie went on to college. Peter went to trade school to learn computers, and Carole became a housewife and mother.

In time, the kids were all married and settled down. Charlie had our first grandchild, a son, who we adored. Peter came next with a granddaughter, and then Carole had twins. We were so blessed with all the grandchildren.

We had family dinners, and every birthday and holiday we were together at one of the houses. Charlie had the larger home of the kids, but Carole had the loveliest backyard. We enjoyed barbecues over there. Her flowerbeds were always full of vibrant colors, and in the summertime, her vegetable garden was over-flowing with crops.

"You sure have a green thumb," I'd say to her.

"Got it from Daddy," she responded.

As a parent, the most joy comes from your children when they're happy and healthy. Charles and I were ecstatic.

IT WAS during one of our family gatherings at Carole's that she dropped a bombshell on us. Her husband had joined the military. They were young and struggling financially, so the service was probably a good choice. But now, I was going to worry about her being alone raising twins while he went off to basic training.

"It'll only be for six weeks, and then we'll be joining him," she said matter-of-factly.

And so began our next trial as a family. Carole would be leaving our town and our close-knit group. We vowed to not let the distance keep us apart, but over time, with age and health issues, traveling to see her and her family became more and more challenging.

ONE EVENING, after a pleasant time at Peter's, I brought up my idea of taking a road trip.

"I really miss Carole," I said.

Charles nodded.

"Maybe we could take a trip." I blurted.

Charles cocked his head toward me, giving me his full attention.

I rattled off the details I had in my mind. "We could take a road trip, visit the kids, and maybe end up in Iowa."

Charles took me into his arms and stared into my eyes. He knew me so well. "A road trip sounds nice," he said rocking me back and forth.

A tear formed in my bottom eyelid. I loved that he knew me so well. I could never keep any secrets from him. "I just thought maybe we could visit some places on our bucket list."

He furrowed his brow, "My bucket list or yours?"

I gently kissed him on the cheek, pulled back and turned away from the embrace. "Mine."

He stepped toward me. I could feel him at my back. He nuzzled into my neck and whispered in my ear.

"Let's take a trip out to Iowa," he said as nonchalantly as if he'd just asked me to go to the movies or the store. "We can also stop and visit Carole and her family along the way," Charles added.

Hearing that idea perked me up. It had been a couple of years since we had seen them. I knew that Carole's twins were in middle school by now, and I was anxious to visit them.

I called the kids and told them our news. They were all excited about our trip. They knew it had been a while since the two of us had taken a vacation. I sugarcoated the reason for the journey; I didn't want them contacting me every day with, "Did you find out anything?"

I merely mentioned that we'd be stopping in Iowa as well. Of course, Carole picked up on that right away —almost as quickly as her father.

"You know, Mom..." she started.

"I know, dear. I plan on turning over some stones while we're there. I certainly don't have any high expectations. Whatever happens is meant to be," I said.

"Yep, I totally get it. Just go there, do some digging, and see what it brings up. BUT," she hollered. "You better tell me as soon as you know something interesting," she said laughing in the receiver.

I let her know our itinerary and when she could expect us to roll into her neck of the woods. She was happy we were stopping by. I wouldn't miss stopping in and seeing her for anything. We talked on the phone weekly, but it wasn't the same. I missed not having her close by, but I was old school, and I believed your place was with your husband.

Charles and I closed up the business and the house. We didn't know how long we'd be gone. The kids would check in on things, but for the most part, we were going to be gone indefinitely. I knew with Charles by my side we'd uncover as much as possible. I grew excited about the possibilities. I also knew that not all the news would be good, and I expected that. I was ready. I was ready for whatever. At least, that's what I told myself.

During our last night at the house, the reality of what we were about to do set in. I was feeling a bit agitated and snapped at Charles.

"Maybe we're making a big mistake. It's not too late. Let's just stop this crazy idea."

Charles rarely got angry, but the look on his face told me maybe I was about to witness a first time.

He grabbed my arm, not hurting me, but getting my attention. "Where is this coming from," he said with a raised voice.

I started crying. I was an emotional mess. Maybe I didn't want to know the truth. "I may be in for news I don't even want to know," I said in between sobs.

He pulled me close. "I'm going to be with you all the way. If it ever gets to be too much, and you want to stop, we'll stop."

I hugged him tightly. Charles was my rock.

CHAPTER 7

OUR FIRST STOP: Las Vegas with all of its flashing neon lights.

I remembered being there before as a child. I recalled the hours I sat in the backseat playing with my doll while my parents were in the casino playing cards. I removed that unpleasant thought from my brain and focused on all the beautiful lights and buildings instead.

Charles found a hotel on the outskirts of town, and we called it an evening. The next day would be long, but we both were excited to see what the Great Salt Lake looked like. But first, a quick stop at the Grand Canyon that was breathtaking and worth every fleeting minute. Then we were on our way to see Carole and the family in Idaho.

As I ᴋɴᴇᴡ she'd do, Carole rolled out the red carpet for us. We loved catching up with her and the family. Carole and I got caught up. I missed having her around to talk with.

Spending time with them was what I'd been missing, though I tried to never show it. Although her husband was away serving our great country, she was an excellent wife and mother.

After an all too short, three-day visit, it was time to hit the road again.

"Now you two be careful," she called out to us as we drove away.

I smiled and nodded, waving to them until I couldn't see them anymore.

Smiling ear to ear, Charles said, "I enjoyed our visit. And the kids are so well-behaved," he went on.

I reached up and wiped the one lonely tear that made its way from my lower lid to my cheek.

"Yes, I did too" was all I could manage to say.

The only way to stop feeling sad about leaving Carole was to concentrate on our next stop—Yellowstone National Park.

I'd READ numerous articles about Yellowstone. I was excited about seeing it, and deep down inside, I hoped we would see some bears and other wild animals.

It was eerily quiet in the cabin that night. Occasionally, Spunky would walk over to the door and sniff under it as if he could smell other animals. My vivid imagination almost got the best of me as I imagined bears, buffalo, and other wild animals right outside our cabin door.

I finally drifted off to sleep where my dreams were more about what I was going to find when we arrived in Iowa than wild animals outside our cabin door.

As we drove along the winding roads that would lead us to the iconic spot of Old Faithful, I was amazed by all the unspoiled land and the beautiful floribunda that draped the dramatic landscape. The area looked like a beautiful painting or photograph. No wonder Wyoming cherished this park. It was spectacular.

After a good night's sleep, we were on our way to the next stop; the Black Hills of South Dakota. I assumed my role as the co-pilot and tried not to dwell on leaving Carole and the family.

To say Mount Rushmore is awesome or breath-taking is an understatement. It was even more gigantic than I thought it would be, and the image of its grandeur left an impression on me that I still hold to this day.

That night I tried to sleep but couldn't, I could hear the soft snores from both the dog and Charles. I chuckled to myself thinking how silly they sounded, at the same time wishing I too could fall asleep. Before long, my eyelids became heavy, and I drifted off to sleep. I don't know what time it was, but before I knew it, I was being awoken by Charles letting me know we needed to hit the road.

"Hey, sleepyhead it's time to get up," he said lightly tapping me on the shoulder.

I stretched my arms wide and let out a moan letting him know I didn't get enough sleep.

"What time is it?" I asked.

"Time to get a move on. We have a long day ahead of us. I'd like to make Iowa before dark," he added as he gathered our things into piles near the door.

"Ok, just give me a few minutes," I pleaded.

He reached down and gave me a peck on the cheek. Every morning for the past thirty years or more, he'd given me a kiss and told me he loved me. "I'm going to take Spunky for a walk. It'll give you time to get ready."

I nodded my head and moaned a bit more as I

stumbled into the bathroom. I looked in the mirror and saw bloodshot and puffy eyes; a sign I didn't sleep well. I splashed cold water on my face, grabbed a washcloth, and used it as a compress trying to get the swelling down. After a few moments, I finished up in the bathroom and got dressed. I was ready to go when the two of them returned from their walk.

"I'm hungry. I need coffee too," I appealed.

"Ok, let's get the car loaded. McDonald's or Burger King?"

"Let's live precariously. Burger King," I said laughing.

We both ate in silence with only the occasional sounds of chewing and slurping hot coffee as noise. Spunky was interested in our food as well. Even though I knew it wasn't healthy for him to have human food, I gave him a couple of pieces of bacon and some of my egg as a reward for being an outstanding traveler.

I REMEMBERED when we got Spunky. He was the runt of the litter, and Carole wouldn't leave without him. A Terrier mix, Spunky was the spitting image of my aunt's dog by the same name.

I clearly recalled the day. I was about six years old, and I was so excited about our visit to Aunt Margie's house. I had been told they'd gotten a new addition to their family, a dog.

I ran as fast as I could into her house to see the little dog. Little did I know, he wasn't fond of children. Before they could stop me, I was in the house, sitting on the couch and petting the little dog. Aunt Margie couldn't believe her eyes. From that day on, Spunky and I were inseparable.

When our family adopted a pup that looked so much like Spunky, we decided to name him the same. It seemed fitting, and the children loved the name.

The closer we got to Sioux City the more nervous I became. I guess it held too many sad memories for me to be happy. I was hoping it would feel different. I mean I did have some happy moments. They were just too few and too far between and almost all of them had to do with Daddy.

I forced myself to recall some of the happier moments. The homemade sled Daddy had made, my days of running in the park with my best friend, even the days in the pool hall, listening to music, and watching my parents shoot pool when I stayed up way too late for a child my age, and meeting my aunt's Spunky for the first time.

Charles could sense I was no longer looking at scenery, but deep in thought. "You ok?"

I nodded, "Just thinking about some stuff."

"It's going to be ok," he said touching my hand.

I studied his face. He was telling the truth. He's been with me all the way, and everything would be ok. I relaxed my shoulders.

"Let's finish up breakfast and get on the road," I said eagerly.

Charles reached over and patted me on the leg. "That's my girl."

ALL WE COULD SEE WERE acres of growing crops—mainly corn. That was our constant landscape for miles and miles. It was a vast canvas with only a palette of neutral and yellow colors that began to run into each other like frames on a camera with only the occasional farmhouse, tractor, or scarecrow to break up the monotony. This was America's farmland.

We passed several little roadside fruit and vegetable stands. They were almost as impressive as California's. I convinced Charles to stop. While he walked Spunky, I picked out a couple of peaches, some fresh corn, and some tomatoes.

Charles put the fresh produce in our little ice chest in the back of the car, and we were off. We'd be arriving at Sioux Falls in just a few hours.

"Just rows and rows of corn," Charles said as he tried to find a radio station.

"Yep. Living here, you'd be in a world of hurt if you didn't like corn," I chuckled.

"It's good for you that I love corn," he said laughing. "How many ways can you fix corn?" He quickly asked, trying to keep the conversation going. It had been a long, boring drive through Nebraska and Iowa.

"Well, the most popular way is boiling it. But in California, we grill everything, so that's my preference.

"Yeah, I like all the vegetables grilled. A little olive oil, salt, and pepper, and hmm good," he said. "Are you about ready for a rest stop?"

"I could stretch my legs," I said re-positioning myself in the car seat.

We stopped and were not the only ones eager to get out and stretch our legs, Spunky was too. He sniffed every garbage can and tree trunk before finally settling on a place to do his business. Then we were on our way again.

"I estimate we'll be pulling into Sioux City in about two hours," Charles, the navigator said.

I looked over at my husband and smiled. Even at fifty-seven, he was as handsome as he was the day we got married. His hair was now grayer, but he had the same laugh lines and wrinkles I had.

CHAPTER 8

CHARLES and I found a quaint little motel for our first night in Sioux City. Our plan was to find a more permanent housing situation, but the motel would do for now. It was clean, with the basics, and that was good enough. The desk clerk was very friendly, so what the hotel lacked in shine, the staff made up for.

We asked about good places to get dinner. The clerk had several recommendations, but we settled on Denny's because Charles wanted breakfast for dinner. I was good with that as well.

Returning to the motel, Charles walked Spunky. Then we did what all travelers do after a long day in a car, we fell into bed exhausted. As tired as I felt, I didn't sleep well that first night. It didn't have anything to do with our accommodations. There were too many things running through my head. And, although it had been years since I set foot in the state, I swear it felt familiar.

I finally drifted off to sleep and woke to the smell of freshly brewed coffee and donuts.

"Oh, that aroma is wonderful," I said in between yawns.

"I stepped out since you were still asleep. The clerk told me of a bakery just down the road. I got fresh apple fritters and a newspaper," he said with a twinkle in his eye.

Over coffee and fritters, we looked over the newspaper. I was looking at the local section of the paper, and Charles was looking at the real estate section.

We'd agreed that it would be best to try to rent a small bungalow that allowed pets so that we could take our time, and at the same time be as comfortable as possible.

"This one sounds promising. One bedroom, one bath, with a fenced in backyard near Chester Park," he read aloud as he took out his pen and began circling a few of the ads.

I smiled. "Near the park would be nice. I remember that park. I used to go there a lot."

Charles looked at me, blinked a couple of times and then went back to looking at houses for rent.

"The only other house I see is on W. 2nd Street. Do you know where that is?"

I shook my head. "I think it's downtown."

"I'll call about the Chester Park house right now," he said as he reached for the phone.

IT WAS a quaint little bungalow built in the 50's, long after I moved away. In fact, I recalled an empty lot where the house now stood.

We knew almost instantly we'd take the house. It was perfect for us and for our mission. It had all the requirements—a bedroom, a bathroom, and a fenced in yard for Spunky, and it was completely furnished.

We told the property owner we'd take it, signed the papers, paid the deposit, and got the keys.

We unloaded the few possessions we brought with us, and I made a list of the items we'd need. I knew a town of this size would have a Wal-Mart.

"You go ahead and get the shopping done. I'll stay with Spunky. He needs to get used to his new space."

Reaching down, I gave Spunky a pat on the head and turned to give Charles a kiss on the cheek.

He turned slightly, and our lips touched. I started to pull away after a quick peck, but he held our kiss, and something about it felt different. He pulled me in close, and the kiss became passionate. It seemed an odd time for this to be happening, but I went with it. I kissed him back, and he was leading me into the bedroom. "So much for the shopping," I whispered as I tossed the list onto the coffee table.

I HADN'T SET foot in this town in over 40 years, yet I still felt I knew my way around. I drove right to the Wal-Mart, even though it had not even existed when I lived there. Later, Charles and I discussed how I had driven right to the supercenter. He chalked it up to me being aware of my surroundings and knowing the direction the downtown area and shopping would most likely be. I nodded my head. I guess he had a valid point.

As I walked up and down the aisles looking for the items on my list, I couldn't help wondering if anyone would recognize me. How would someone recognize me after all this time?

I felt a bit anxious about being in the store by myself. I don't know why. Maybe I thought someone would run up to me and say, "Patsy. Is that you?"

I had an excellent memory, which made me a great

private detective. I could remember things that happened when I was three and four years old. Why was it so outside the realm of possibilities that I would recognize someone from my past? After all, many people from small towns such as this never leave.

I finally finished my shopping and got up to the checkout counter to pay for my things. As the young lady rang up my items, I searched her face for details, for a resemblance to anyone I might have known. She smiled at me. I smiled back. We made small chitchat about the weather, and when the last item was placed in my bag, I decided to be bold.

"Have you lived here long?" I asked.

"All my life," she answered.

"So, your family has been here for a long time?"

"For as long as I can remember," she said as she handed me my change.

"Well, it's a lovely town. I'm new. We just moved in."

"Where are you living?" She asked.

"We just rented a little bungalow across from the park."

"Oh, I know right where you mean. My family knows the owners."

I smiled. Not sure, of what else to say, I gathered up my bags and placed them back into the cart.

"Have a great day," I said as I headed out the automatic glass doors.

My heart was beating fast as I loaded the bags into the trunk. If this is how it was going to feel when we began to poke around, I'd better get used to it. There were many deep-seated secrets in this town regarding my birth. I didn't want to get anyone in trouble; I just wanted to know the truth. Was Lyle my real dad (like Irma had hinted at when she mentioned he'd been promiscuous) or was my adoption just a cover-up for a family member who'd been careless?

I knew Charles was just as anxious as I was about finding out the truth. He would have never committed to this adventure if he didn't believe that solving this mystery would help me somehow. I loved that he loved me that much.

For our first night in the new house, we made hot dogs and chili for dinner. Afterward, we settled into the evening by reading. I was reading a new romance, and Charles was reading a detective book.

"Tomorrow, I'll get the phone hooked up. We'll need it," he added turning the page to his book.

"Ok, that sounds great."

After reading a few pages, I drifted off to sleep. I dreamed about the time when I was a little girl, and we were at my Aunt and Uncles farm. The chickens were chasing me, and my mom grabbed one of them and rang its neck so we could have it for supper. Watching that caused me to lose my appetite. They all laughed at me and told me I was a crybaby. What I remember most, though, was how readily my mother killed that poor chicken. That apparent cruelty was burned into my memory.

CHAPTER 9

THE NEXT MORNING, we made the trip to the telephone company and afterward, went for lunch. Charles said it was a good way to get to know our surroundings. We ordered sandwiches and fries and sipped on freshly brewed iced tea. As we ate, we went over our strategy regarding the search for information about my parents.

We agreed the first thing we'd do was go to the old neighborhood where the pool hall was.

We'd lived in a few places in that town, and we planned to check them all out. Charles also wanted to drive by the farm where my aunt and uncle lived. We'd looked up my maiden name in the telephone book and saw several families with the name. Charles said we could do some cold calling. I was a little afraid of that, but I followed his lead.

He looked up from his plate and stared into my eyes. "This reminds me of the days when we were hitting the pavement," he said eagerly. I could see the enthusiasm in his eyes.

I smiled. "We're the perfect duo for this," I agreed remembering what a fantastic team we were.

His grin told the entire story. Charles was enjoying our new adventure.

As we made our way across town toward the pool hall, another memory surfaced. Next door to it had been another building with a dance hall upstairs. On weekends, my parents and their friends, with kids in tow, would go there. As the parents danced, we children would sit around and play jacks, and watch our parents laugh and be loud. I wondered if the old building was still there.

With the map on my lap, I highlighted the area we were looking for, and when we arrived at the address where the pool hall had been, Charles slowly drove by. It looked all different. I checked the map and notes to make sure we were in the right place. Nothing looked the way I remembered it.

"According to the map, this is it," I said. Nothing looked the same.

"Are you sure?" He said as he continued driving.

He made a U-turn and headed back to the gas station. He pulled into the parking lot and parked the car.

I got out and looked around trying to get my bearings. Nothing looked the same. I closed my eyes and attempted to picture our apartment, and the building next door to us.

I tried to remember what was across the street and down the block.

With my hands blocking the sun from my eyes, I searched the area looking for clues.

"I remember a large hill that was behind my house. We used to go sledding on it."

I walked to the other side of the gas station to try to see it. It was there but didn't appear as big as I'd remembered it.

Charles followed me. "Children sometimes remember things as being bigger, or even small than they actually were," he said trying to calm me.

"Across the street is where my best friend, Lisa lived," I said pointing to a three-story apartment building that now stood in place of her home.

"They tore everything down," I said sadly.

"That's progress for you," Charles muttered as he reached out to take my hand.

A tear formed in my eye, and I brushed it away. It was too soon for tears. We'd only just started the search.

We drove out to the last address I had for Uncle George and Aunt Toot's farmhouse. There among rows of corn stood an old farmhouse. The paint was peeling from the boards and the front porch that had seen better days. The old farmhouse was much smaller than I remembered.

We drove up to the front of the house and got out of the car. Before either of us could step foot onto the porch, the screen door flew open, and a sour-looking woman about my age wearing an apron stared at us.

"H-h-hello," I stammered.

She stood stone cold saying nothing.

"Hi, wondered if you could help us. We're looking for some folks," Charles said.

"Who might that be?" She replied curtly.

Charles looked at me, and then he directed his attention back to the woman on the porch. "The Bowmans. We're looking for the Bowman family."

She looked at me, and then she looked at Charles.

"There's no one here by that name," she said, and as quickly as she came out, she went back inside, slamming the screen door shut behind her.

Charles took my hand. I was shaking, and he knew very well that this incident had upset me.

"I don't think she's telling the truth, but we'll let it go—for now," he said as we walked toward the car.

We drove in silence for a while. Finally, I had, to say something. "What makes you think she's not telling the truth?"

"Well for one, she wasn't very friendly. Most Iowans are very friendly. She wanted to get rid of us. You'd usually pick up on that, Pat. You have excellent investigative and instinctive skills," he added smiling.

"You're right. I felt her uneasiness with our presence. I suppose it's too close to home."

"That's okay, that's why you brought me along," he said, gently squeezing my hand.

"We may be searching for a needle in a haystack, Charles. Aunt Toots and Uncle George had left Iowa before we did. That old farmhouse has probably changed owners a zillion times," I said looking out the car window at row after row of corn. Charles just kept driving.

"See all these rows of corn? We used to run and hide among the stalks. We were dirt poor, but we had so much fun in those days. We didn't know we were poor or, at least if we did, we didn't care," I said, smiling about the days I played on the farm.

Sometimes, I felt Charles couldn't relate to my stories. His family had been pretty well off. His dad was a big shot in the car industry in Michigan. Charles was educated and had military experience. I felt like a dumb farm girl from Iowa by comparison.

"I realize that maybe the lady doesn't know anything about your family, but I still think in a small town such as this, stories still float around or are passed down from family to family. I think she might know a little something."

I turned to him, and although his eyes remained on the road, I spoke to his face. "Whenever you say enough is enough I'll be ready to leave too."

He cut his face sharply to look at me. "We just got here, Pat. Give it time. Besides, we're retired now. This is for fun. Relax. Take a chill pill," he said laughing.

Although he didn't see it, I nodded.

"Let's look for the convent," I said with the enthusiasm I knew he wanted.

I FELT nervous as we entered the building. I'm not sure why, except that we were about to find out some things that maybe I did not want to know.

Just inside, we were greeted by a smiling young nun dressed in the habit of her order. She introduced herself as Sister Mary Margaret.

"Hello, how can I help you?" I gently nudged Charles. I wasn't sure I had the courage to ask the difficult questions yet.

"Hello, we're hoping you can help us," he smoothly replied. "My wife," he said nodding in my direction, "has some information that shows her adoptive mother perhaps once lived here as a teen," Charles said, presenting a copy of the document.

The sister took the paper and looked it over. She seemed to stare at it for a long time. She looked up at us, first at me, and then at Charles.

"We keep records of everyone who's lived here. At one time, we were an orphanage and housed many children. It could be that your mother," she said glancing over at me, "was in our orphanage and the census doesn't clearly show that."

I spoke up. "My mother told me she was a nun here at this convent." Then I added, "In fact, many family members corroborated that as well."

Charles gently rubbed my arm. "What she means, is, this is the only piece of information we have, and we aren't sure if there is any value. That's what we are trying to determine," Charles said looking over at me.

The sister looked at me for a long time. "Well, if that's true, we'll have records stating that as well. Do you have a telephone number? This information will take some time to gather. I'll contact you as soon as I have something."

We gave the sister our newly assigned telephone number and thanked her for her time.

On the drive back to our bungalow, Charles asked me again about my mother and her being a nun.

"Now, how is it that the story developed about your mother being a nun?"

I shook my head. "It's beyond me how she could be. She was so mean and evil. But that's the story I remember someone telling me, and for the life of me, not sure who?" I said.

"We had wooden crosses that hung on the walls of our house; we blessed all our meals, and we said prayers before going to bed at night. Sundays we'd all go to church, but by Sunday evening, the gang would be drinking, cursing and playing cards. Talk about hypocrisy," I added.

"Well, as much of a cover-up as your adoption has been—from discovering you on a bed in their home to hints about your dad's indiscretions, I'd say maybe it was more likely Irma lived in a convent because she was homeless," Charles said matter-of-factly.

I shot him a look that told him he may be on to something. "That does make more sense," I agreed.

"Families have a way of glorifying things or embellishing to make them easier to believe or accept," he said.

I thought about what he said. "Yes, and children sometimes don't remember everything exactly correct," I said looking over at him.

I got what he was saying. He was trying to tell me, in a nice way, that either I remembered the nun story wrong, or my family lied to me.

"Well, I'm ready for whatever the sister finds out," I finally said.

"Let's go to the newspaper office tomorrow. There might be more articles regarding your mysterious appearance in your parents' house." He had a good idea. Maybe more than one story had run on the mysterious appearance of Baby Jane Doe. After all, that was big news in a small town back then.

THE NEXT DAY Charles and I hit the road to the newspaper office.

We entered the office, and a pleasant woman in her fifties offered her assistance.

As Charles spoke to her, I noticed her features. She had twinkly blue eyes, and when she smiled, she had tiny laugh lines around her eyes and her mouth. Her brown hair had touches of gray in streaks much like my own. Something about her seemed familiar.

"My wife and I are trying to locate articles about a baby found in a residence sometime around the summer of 1929."

The woman looked at me. I smiled. She looked back at Charles. He cleared his throat.

"This is the one article we do have, but we believe there may be others," he said handing it to the woman to read.

After she had finished reading it, she looked back at me.

"We keep all the articles written on microfiche, and we also have a database on the computer. Have you checked the local library as well?" She asked looking at Charles then at me.

"Not yet. This is just the first of many stops for us."

"This will take some time. Do you live in town?"

Charles scribbled our telephone number on a pad that was on the counter and pushed it toward the woman.

"Great. I'll contact you in a few days."

"Thanks for your time," Charles said.

"Yes. Thanks for your time," I echoed.

Hand in hand we walked out to our parked car.

"Geez, another callback. I was hoping she would look for something while we waited," Charles said disgustedly.

"Something about that woman seemed familiar," I said.

"Maybe you went to school with her. She's about your age," Charles queried.

"What's our next plan of action?" I asked still trying to remain optimistic.

"Find a restaurant. I'm hungry," he said, starting the engine.

OVER CLUB SANDWICHES and delicious iced tea, Charles and I talked about our children and wondered how everyone was doing. It had been a few days since we'd spoken to them.

"Have you called the kids recently?" Charles asked.

"I will in a few days. We don't have anything to report yet."

Smiling, Charles nodded. "No news is good news," he added.

"There have to be some relatives still alive in this town, or nearby. Not everyone moved to California, correct?" Charles asked.

"No, and my aunts and uncles never moved back to Iowa after moving to California. To my knowledge, my mother and half-sister were the only ones to go back, and Irma's family was originally from Texas. If the nun can't give us any more information regarding my mother's stay at the convent, it may be a dead end."

"Not necessarily. Your sister got married, correct?"

"Yes. She was married and had a son."

"Aha, another lead," he smiled and munched on his sandwich.

CHAPTER 11

IT BOTHERED me that my dad's pool hall and Lisa's house were no longer standing. If Charles worried about it, he didn't let on. He was already looking for the next clue.

After a couple of days, the woman from the newspaper office contacted us. She'd found another article for us to read. We headed over right away to get a copy of it.

Arriving at the newspaper office, the woman finished with another customer and then handed me the clipping, "This is what I found."

I took the newspaper clipping out of her hand and read aloud, "Mystery Tot's Mother. Identity of the woman who abandoned babe not disclosed. Steps to legally adopt the child however, will be taken immediately. Mrs. Bowman told a Journal reporter Tuesday Evening."

I continued, "It also says that Irma knew who the mother was, but didn't want to divulge the information. It went on to say that she knew the child as likable and would take care of it. That was the joke of the century. As likable as I might have been, she was never nice to me. I wonder what changed her mind."

Taking a moment to absorb what I had just read, I said, "This is new information."

The lady at the counter responded, "Good, but this other article we have says she didn't know who my mother was."

I smiled at the lady and pointing to the clipping I told her "Thank you so much for this. "By the way, you look very familiar to me. Do we know one another?"

At that moment, it clicked, she knew it, and so did I.

"Lisa?" I asked.

She smiled and nodded her head.

"Lisa!" I exclaimed. I reached across the counter and gave her a firm hug.

"I can't believe it's you. I thought something about your eyes and your smile seemed familiar. I even said that to Charles the other day," I said looking over at him and smiling.

"I didn't want to say anything to you then. It was strange seeing you. I wasn't quite sure what to say. Especially after you told me what you were here for."

I furrowed my brows. "You knew I was adopted. I told you." I said.

She lowered her head. "Yes, I knew, and I may know someone who can help you."

I stared hard into her eyes. Had I heard her correctly? "Who," I asked.

A smile appeared on her face, "Sioux City is still a small town, even after all these years. I did some checking around, and a name surfaced. I'll give you his number."

I hugged Lisa. She handed me a note with the name Francis Stewart on it and phone number. We made arrangements to meet for lunch later in the week.

Walking hand in hand toward the car, I looked at Charles. "I feel satisfied we've accomplished something for the day. I found Lisa, and we received a new clipping that might give us a new lead," I said looking for a nod.

Charles nodded. "A very productive day, indeed. I'm hungry," he said smiling.

I squeezed his hand, "How about egg salad sandwiches for lunch?"

Charles grin widened. He squeezed my hand in return.

While we ate, Charles looked at the note Lisa had given me, "Looks like Lisa has given us more information and a new lead. This man may have some more information. Does his name sound familiar to you?"

"No, not at all."

"That's alright, Pat. Not every name will be. It can be a lead, though, and we must—"

"I know, follow every lead," I said finishing his sentence. He smiled.

"That's my girl," he said pulling me in for a hug.

"Charles, I hope you know how special you are to me. I know I can be a bit moody sometimes, but I want you to know that I love you and thank God every day you're in my life."

"We make a great team, Pat," he said kissing me lightly.

Later, we received a call from Sister Mary Margaret. She had located some information for us and asked us to come to the convent.

As we drove the ten miles or so, my mind began to wander back to the winter when I was about four years old, and a homemade sled Daddy had made.

All the other children had store-bought sleds, and I had nothing. We were dirt poor, so a store-bought sled was out of the question. My dad went into the garage and made me a toboggan type sled out of sheet metal and rope. Once the kids saw how fast I could slide down a hill, they all wanted to try it too. I was the most popular kid on the hill that day. I smiled at the memory of my dad.

"PLEASE, LET'S GO IN HERE," the sister said, directing us down a hallway that led to a large room. Our footsteps echoed as we entered the sparsely furnished room. There was only a large wooden desk placed near the center of the room, two chairs, and a large Bible on a wooden stand that faced a lovely stained-glass window. Beyond the window lay a serene courtyard. It was a beautiful setting.

We sat down as directed and the sister took a seat behind the desk. She cleared her throat before taking out a piece of paper, which she placed on her desk, turned it, and gently slid it closer so we could read it. All I could see at first was a bunch of names and ages on it. I quickly scanned it for something familiar when she began to talk.

"I'm sorry. It took me longer than I thought it would to locate the information. But, I wanted to make sure it would be useful and of course, accurate. Although we keep records of all children who've passed through our doors, finding the documents can sometimes take a while," she said smiling at us.

I could feel my heart beating in my chest, and I wondered if anyone else could hear it. My palms grew moist in anticipation of the news. Finally, she spoke.

"Based on the 1910 census information you provided, I was able to find a match. It does appear that a young woman with a child came to the convent seeking refuge approximately in the fall of 1910."

She reached into her folder and produced another document.

"This record shows the young woman left the child with us, but it was only to be temporary."

"Temporary? Do you mean she was to come back for the child but never did?" I asked.

"It appears the arrangement was that once she got a job, secured an apartment, etc. she was going to come back for the child."

"It says all of that in the file?" I asked, gesturing to the manila folder she held in her hand.

The sister looked at me with sad eyes.

"Yes. It says that the approximate age of the older one is between sixteen to eighteen years old."

"The younger one?"

"The younger one, about four or five," she replied.

I paused a moment. Trying to let the new information sink in. I looked deeply into the sister's eyes. "On one of the census's it just says M and P. Initials, I suppose. Do you have any information regarding that?" I asked searching for clues.

"M was for Mary and P for Priscilla," she said reading off the file.

"Mary, I can understand. I have a census that shows my dad, Lyle and Mary listed as occupants. I'm pretty sure my adoptive mother Irma used Mary on some legal documents."

The sister nodded she comprehended what I was saying. "Yes, unfortunately, occupants frequently gave different names at different times, making the information hard to validate. Sometimes they used nicknames, middle names as first, and so on."

"I'm finding that out. I have one that says my name is Patsy and one that says my name is Patricia."

Sister Mary Margaret nodded. "It appears as you got older your name reappeared to what you were born with. It's like Debra and Debbie, Catherine and Cathy," she added.

Pushing her chair out from the desk, she offered her hand to Charles and then to me letting us know the meeting was over.

"Sometimes children are born out of wedlock, and that could be why you still had her last name. Perhaps there was another young woman with the same last name; a sister, cousin; another relative?"

"She was from Texas, and Brown is a very common name," I said agreeing with her there must be more to this than it seemed.

Charles hadn't said much during the visit. However, just before our meeting was adjourned, he did ask one compelling question.

"By any chance, are there any photos of this "M. Brown" that we could look at?"

The sister stared at Charles, not blinking an eyelash. She cleared her throat softly. "We do have some pictures archived here." Opening a folder, she took out a glossy picture and slid it across the desk toward me.

I stared at the image. It was a young woman of about sixteen years old, just like the sister had said. By her side, was a child approximately five years old. It was hard to see their faces. The picture was timeworn and had seen better days. The quality of the image was another issue.

"I can't quite make out their features. The older girl could be Irma, but who is the younger one?" I said staring at every inch of the picture, trying to find any clue.

"Is there any way we could get a copy of this?" Charles asked.

"You may have it. We have three pictures from that day," the sister replied.

We thanked her for the information, and with the photo in hand, we departed the convent and rode home in silence.

CHAPTER 12

WHEN WE GOT BACK to our little bungalow, I went straight into the kitchen and started a pot of coffee. I was banging cupboards and clanking cups when Charles entered the kitchen.

"I know you're upset. It may not have been the news you were hoping for, but it's a lead. We're not throwing in the towel because of what the sister told us," he said turning me around to face him.

A tear started to roll down my cheek. I shuddered a little when he brought me in close for a much-needed hug.

"Don't cry, Pat. We've just begun to touch the tip of the iceberg."

I loved how he always made comparisons of our trials and tribulations to old clichés. Realizing he was right, I pulled myself together and was finishing making the coffee when the phone rang. Charles answered, and I heard quiet mumbling from the other room.

"Pat, the phone is for you, it's Lisa," he called out.

I dried my hands and rushed to the phone, "Lisa, I am so glad to hear from you."

"Are we still on for lunch?" she asked in her bubbly voice.

"I'd love that. Where shall we meet?" I asked.

"This is so nice ... us having lunch together. I've thought about you so many times over the years," she said while she wiped the sweat from her glass.

"Seems so long ago. Pool hall, apartment, you across the street," I stammered.

"Do you remember the time you rescued that family from gas fumes?" She asked.

I'd totally forgotten about that. All of a sudden, the memory came crashing through. They were Lisa's next-door neighbors, a young couple with an infant.

Lisa and I accompanied her mother when she went to see the new baby. It was wintertime, and the heater was on in the house. One by one, the occupants started feeling dizzy and sick. I knew something was happening. I quickly grabbed the infant and ran out the front door, collapsing on the stoop. I woke up in the Smithfield's home with everyone swooning over me.

Looking her straight in the eyes, I said, "Wow, I forgot about that."

Smiling she said, "Yep, you were the citizen of the year after performing that heroic act. If it hadn't been for your sharp observation and fast acting, we'd all have been dead."

"I realize everyone got out, but we never talked about exactly what happened that day," I said looking for answers.

"After we saw you grab the baby, it all made sense what was going on. We followed you out the door. I almost dropped to the ground too." Then she added, "That baby was so lucky."

"So, tell me, how did you come to be working at the newspaper office?"

"Well, my family has owned the paper for about thirty years. So, I started out writing obituaries, progressed to news stories, and now, I help with the counter," she said taking a bite of her salad.

How about you? What do you and your husband do?

"Well, my husband—Charles, and I own a private

investigation service. We're mostly retired now, but we still have the business."

"Just like Magnum P.I.?" She asked with a giggle.

"We've had some fascinating clients, and it was pretty exciting in our youth. Like everything, age has transformed it some. We still try to find missing persons and follow husbands and wives, but the really strange stuff ... well, we leave that to the younger investigators."

She nodded. "What about the time you got locked in the freezer in that old warehouse?" She asked.

An eerie feeling came over me as I relived that day. "I don't know what I was thinking going back alone, and then getting inside the darn thing," I said disgustedly.

Lisa nodded. "We were all young and dumb," she said laughing. "I'm just glad your daddy went looking for you," she added.

"Me too," I said. "Daddy got concerned because I hadn't come home by the time I should have and went out looking for me. For some reason, he checked the warehouse. When he saw that old freezer, he opened it up and found me locked inside. When he pulled me out, I was red in the face with sweat dripping from my forehead and temples. He took a switch to my behind all the way home."

"What possessed you to go back alone the next day?" Lisa asked.

"I suppose, I was curious. I remember after I got inside and couldn't get out that I was rather calm. I tried kicking the top and screaming. After a while, I just gave up," I said solemnly.

"Why do you suppose you gave up?" She asked.

"Maybe I just knew my daddy would find me. I don't know. I just remember feeling calm and at peace."

"It still gives me goose bumps just thinking about what could have happened," Lisa said.

LISA DROVE ME BACK HOME. "Don't be a stranger," she called out as she drove away.

Charles was sitting on the couch with Spunky when I came in.

"Did you have a nice lunch?" He said looking up from the yellow legal pad he was writing on.

"We did. We did a lot of reminiscing. She reminded me of a lot of things I'd forgotten about," I said, leaning down giving him a peck on the cheek.

"Like what?" He asked.

"Just kid stuff. Nothing to help us with what we're

doing. In fact, we didn't even talk about that. Strange, huh?" I called out from the kitchen.

"Well, I spoke to Francis Stewart. We're going to meet him at Cindy's coffee shop tomorrow.

"That's interesting," I said plopping down next to him on the couch. "I'm nervous about meeting him."

"Nothing to be nervous about, Pat. You're with me, and I'm not going to let anything happen to you. You know that, right?" He added.

"When I was younger the adrenalin would be pumping a mile a minute with this type of adventure. Now, I'm just nervous," I said trying to explain my emotion.

THE FOLLOWING DAY we drove to Cindy's coffee shop. It was more of a diner. It had lots of glass windows that looked out to a rather busy street. Its location was ideal. We weren't sure what Francis would look like, so I scoured the place looking for an older man with glasses and short hair. I don't know why. I just thought that's what he'd look like. I knew he wouldn't be holding up a sign saying: Phillips Family. That much I was sure of.

The diner was busy, and only a few seats remained unoccupied. Just as we were about to give up, thinking perhaps we'd been sent on a wild goose chase, a short man with glasses and graying hair approached Charles.

"Are you Charles?" He asked.

Charles and I looked at one another, and then we both nodded. The man led us to a table he had secured in the back corner. Charles and I sat next to one another with Francis sitting across from Charles.

After we ordered some coffee, Charles engaged Francis in a conversation about local events, sports, and the weather. I had learned early on that part of being a good detective is to get your source softened up, so they spill the beans later. Charles was doing just that.

"I knew your sister, Patsy."

Those words stumbled around inside my brain for a few seconds while I digested what I'd heard. Finally, I said, "Oh."

"I dated her after her husband passed away," he added, hoping that would get me to say more.

"Husband passed away?" I repeated, looking at Charles then back to Francis.

"Eddie Spencer was his name."

"Does this mean Teresa is still alive?" I queried.

"Yes, she is. She's in a convalescent home. However, she's been diagnosed with a rare bone disease and unable to walk. Her son—"

"Does her son live here too?" I interjected.

"No. I believe James moved to Texas," he responded.

"What happened to her husband?" I asked.

"He abused alcohol and passed away several years ago," Francis said.

Softening my face at the news, I asked about her son. "And James, what do you know about him?"

Frances responded, "I believe he is a lawyer."

"I'd like any information you have on James as well," Charles said boldly.

I swallowed. I was ready to ask more questions. "What, if anything, can you tell me about my parents?

"You mean your biological parents?" He asked.

I was about to correct him, when he added, "I know who your real parents are."

I pondered his statement and what it could mean for me. Was I ready to know the truth? I swallowed hard.

Charles looked over at me.

"Hang on just a moment," Charles said, patting my hand lightly to reassure me "Let's give Pat a chance to absorb this."

Francis, realizing he may have coughed up a bit more than we were ready to handle, leaned back in the booth and let out a sigh. "I'm probably a bit overzealous in my approach given that you just started your search and all," he said.

I nodded. Clearing my throat, I asked, "Do you have the address of the convalescent home?"

He scribbled down the address on a bit of paper and slid it across the table.

As I reached for it, he took it back. "You might want her son's information too." He scribbled something else on the paper and moved it back to our side of the table.

"Do you know who my parents were?" I blurted out.

"Yes, I believe so. At least, I know what Teresa told me. However, based on some other information I have found, it may not be true. Unfortunately, she had a habit of not always telling the truth. That's why we broke up. I'll reserve the rest of the information I have until you can confirm or deny some things. We'll meet again," he said looking at Charles and me with a smile before getting up and walking out.

CHAPTER 13

THAT NIGHT, over grilled cheese sandwiches and hot tomato soup, we discussed our plan of action.

"Do you think he's telling the truth? How do we know he's not a bald-faced liar?" I asked tasting my soup.

"If he is, he's a good one," Charles said in between bites. "Truthfully, I think he knows more than he told us. How much more remains to be seen," he said looking me deep in my eyes.

"Well, I trust your instincts better than mine," I murmured. "I'm probably too close to the situation,"

I TRIED to sleep that night, but all I could hear in my

head were the words that my sister and her son were still alive. I wondered if she'd mellowed in her older years, and maybe even got a bit nicer. We'd find out soon enough, I supposed. I tried to close my eyes and rest. I knew I had a big day coming up.

Arriving the next morning at the convalescent hospital, we discovered that it was an older wooden building with wings on both sides of the central building. After parking, we walked through the sliding front doors and approached the front desk. Several people were busy answering phones, looking at charts, and helping other visitors. It resembled a hospital.

"Can I help you?" A pleasant voice asked.

"Yes, my wife and I would like to visit one of the residents. Her name is Teresa Bowman-Spencer. We believe she's a resident here. We're relatives visiting from out of state," he added.

The young attendant looked at a chart and then directed us to room fifteen. We walked down a hallway bustling with activity. There were residents in wheelchairs, nurses pushing medicine carts, and down at one end, we could see the meal cart delivering lunch.

When we got to room fifteen, we paused and then knocked before entering.

The room had two beds, but only one appeared to be in use. The bed closest to the window was neatly made and had a couple of stuffed animals on top. On the built-in dresser top were personal items such as a handheld mirror, brush, comb, and pictures of people. I walked over to look at the photos.

There was one of a young woman with a small child and a man. I assumed it was Teresa and her husband when their family was just starting out. The other picture was of Irma and Teresa during the latter years of Mother's life. No picture of Daddy, and none of me.

"Do you think this is her?" Charles asked pointing at one of the photos.

"Ahem," a voice said behind us.

We both turned around to see a woman in her late seventies in a wheelchair. I could immediately see the resemblance and knew it was her.

"Can I help you with something?" She said in a clipped tone.

"Yes, you can," Charles said. "My name is Charles Phillips, and this is my wife, Patricia. You may have known her as Patsy," he added.

The woman looked at me, paused for about two

seconds, and then shouted, "Why are you here? I don't want to see you. Get out. Get out the both of you. Leave now before I call security."

I started to shake. Charles reached for my hand.

"Listen, there's no reason to get loud or be belligerent. We came in peace. Pat is just trying to find out some things about her childhood. We were hoping you'd help us. But, I can see that is out of the question. So, as you requested, we'll leave."

"What is it you want?" She said through clenched teeth.

"Answers about my mother," I said as calmly as I could.

"You never cared a thing about Irma. Why now?" She growled.

"Are you serious? She was my mother. I always cared about her and wanted her to love me, but she never did. You two had a better relationship than we did, and you weren't her daughter either." I yelled.

"She was more of a mother to me than my own was," Teresa spat. "I took care of her until she died. Where were you?" She snipped.

"I was in California raising a family of my own. Now look, we just have a few questions, and then we'll be gone. Please tell me who my real parents were."

"Lyle and Irma were your parents."

"I don't believe that. Maybe Lyle was my dad, but there is no way in heck Irma was my mother. She detested the very earth I walked on." I said boldly.

She looked at me with narrowed eyes, and spoke in a low, angry tone, "Don't you be coming here trying to stir up old stuff. That was a lot of years ago."

Charles had had enough of the back and forth and not getting anywhere.

"Francis thought you might be able to help us," he said straightforward. "Obviously, he was wrong."

She looked him up and down. She curled her lips and out came the hatred I was accustomed to. Nothing had changed, not even in a seventy-something old woman. "Francis is full of B.S. He doesn't know a thing," she spewed.

"So, is that your final answer? You're not going to give us any information about anything. Not a name, a place, or a date we could investigate further?" Charles said in a challenging tone.

She only growled in response.

As we walked past her toward the door, Charles tossed a business card with our local phone number on it into her lap. "Just in case you change your mind," he said irritably.

We both sat in the car for a few minutes calming

down and gathering our thoughts. I was breathing heavy. Charles took my hand and said, "Take some deep breaths, it'll be ok. That woman knows something."

"I think she does too but doesn't look like she wants to tell me—us," I stammered.

We drove toward home but stopped to pick up some wine and a take-out pizza. It would take more than tomato soup and grilled cheese sandwiches to comfort us that night.

Over the pizza and wine, it was just like old times. We were hunkered down around a coffee table, reviewing what we had learned, and discussing our plan of attack.

"I think we should look up her son," Charles said in his best Magnum P.I.—Tom Selleck voice.

I got a little tipsy on the wine. It did that to me sometimes, especially if I was stressed or overtired. I was both. I started to get a little playful with Charles.

THE NEXT MORNING, we acted like shy, young lovers. We talked about our plans for the day over coffee. "With your permission, I'd like to contact James," Charles asked.

"Ok, that's fine. Go ahead," I said ready for the next step.

But, James would neither take our calls nor respond to the messages we left. We were back to square one.

"So, Pat, what do you want to do? Teresa won't talk to us, and neither will James. That leaves Francis. He's the only one who will."

Nodding my head, I agreed. He was our only link left. "Call him," I said.

We set the appointment up for a couple of days later and then we both agreed that a trip back to the farmhouse was in order as well. Maybe the lady of the house would have a change of heart.

"I KNOW you said you didn't know the Bowman's at all," Charles started off telling the woman who greeted us in the gravel driveway.

"Yep, that's right. I don't know the Bowman's," she spat.

"What about the Browns? Did you know anyone with that last name?" I probed.

The lady just stared at the two of us.

"How long has your family lived here?" I asked.

"Listen, I know what you're doing, and it's not going to work. I told you then, and I'm telling you now. I don't know any Brown's or Bowman's."

I reached out and gently touched her arm. "Ma'am, I'm not attempting to stir up any trouble or bring up undesirable memories. I just want to find my family. Can you help us, please?"

She stopped trying to get away, paused a moment, and turned to face me.

"Come inside," she said in a quiet voice

Charles and I looked at each other. No one had to invite us a second time.

The farmhouse hadn't changed a whole lot since I was a kid. White kitchen cabinets, linoleum on the floor, and a large rock fireplace in the living room told the story of a neglected old house. It even smelled that way, ancient and musty—as if it needed a good airing out.

"Pull up a chair. What would you like? Coffee, tea, or water?" She asked politely.

We both answered coffee at the same time. Seemed she'd mellowed out.

"Louise, what can you tell us, if anything about Pat's family?" Charles asked.

"We were cousins Lyle, Jessie, and me," Louise said grinning.

"So, let me get this straight. You and Pat's dad were cousins?" Charles asked.

Louise nodded her head as she took a sip of her coffee. "Our daddies were brothers," she informed us.

"Mary and I were friends. She'd visit me often, and it seemed she was always timing it for when Lyle was here. One thing led to another, and they were a couple. Quite a scandal them two," she added with a grin.

"Why a scandal?" Charles asked.

"The age difference was one concern, and the second one was because he'd been married before."

"I was close to my daddy's sisters, and of course, Whitey. But now you're telling me Daddy had other relatives too?"

"Well, Whitey was the son of your Aunt Margie's husband from a previous relationship. He wasn't blood kin to you," Louise said dropping yet another bombshell on my head.

"You know, I'd never asked how I was related to Whitey. I was just always told he was my cousin. Seemed there were a lot of second wives and husbands in my family's past," I said.

Then a thought occurred to me, "Was Aunt Margie's husband married to Whitey's mom?"

Shaking her head, Louise confirmed what I already

knew. There was no marriage, just another indiscretion.

"I don't recall seeing any strange women hanging around. Who was she?"

"Well, that's another mystery, dear. You see, he never would confirm who Whitey's mother was. I've heard different names throughout the years, but I don't know for sure."

I thought back to the time Whitey and I had gotten into an argument, and he blurted out that my mother was a whore. It now appeared his mother may have been one as well.

"That's so odd that Aunt Margie never told me that Whitey wasn't her real son. That tells me she was good at keeping secrets just like the rest of the family. Maybe even the one regarding who my real parents were."

"Well, since you didn't know about that little detail, you probably don't know that you also have a half-brother named Thomas," she blurted out.

My palms were getting wet, and I could feel my face burn with redness.

"This brother, was he Teresa's brother or my brother from another mother?" I said, not purposely trying to create a rhyme.

She said grinning, "Different moms. Teresa's mom was a fat pig. Plain and simple. I don't know what Lyle saw in her, but they were married and had Teresa," she confirmed.

"Thomas was several years younger than Teresa. Your daddy sure had some children," she said.

I looked at Charles, "We have to locate Thomas or his mother. That could lead us to my biological mother."

I lowered my eyes briefly. When I raised them, I was looking squarely into Louise's. "Teresa was never kind to me. I wondered why the hate. For a brief time, I even wondered if Teresa could be my mother. Wouldn't that be a twist of fate," I said.

"You know dear, back in the day, it was common for kinfolk to take on babies of unmarried family members and raise them as their own. I don't know if that is the case with your story, but it could be. I don't know why Irma or Teresa was so evil to you, but I had heard through the grapevine that Lyle worshiped the ground you walked on. Maybe they were jealous of his love for you."

"I thought that at first, but something just doesn't add up. If Irma didn't want to adopt me, why didn't she turn me over to the authorities when they reported finding me? Instead, they raised me as their own."

"Maybe Lyle was your real dad," she said candidly.

It was strange how this lady, whom we had now

discovered to be my cousin Louise, had gone from mean and not wanting anything to do with us, to being the most helpful person we had met so far. I just had to know what made her decide to open up.

"Why are you sharing all this information with us now? Before, you were determined not to talk to us. What changed your mind?"

She sighed, "I decided that the secrets had been kept long enough. I mean this 1985. Who cares what people did back in the day? I, for one, don't."

"Do you have any other secrets to reveal?" Charles asked in his best investigator's voice.

"Well, just that I have a couple of addresses you might want to check out," she said as she went into the other room in search of something.

She returned with an address book, sat down, and laid it open on the table. With one hand, she turned the pages, and with the other, she wrote some things down on a piece of paper.

Handing me the piece of paper, she said, "These will probably be useful to you."

WE DROVE to the first address. We pulled up alongside a cemetery. Charles and I took a second glance at the address on the paper and compared it to the street marker. It was the same. We parked the car and walked among the graves. We found a marker that read, "Thomas Bowman."

"Why didn't she tell us he died?" Charles said in disgust.

"I need to talk to Teresa again," I said walking away, but not before taking a picture of the grave marker.

CHAPTER 14

THE NEXT FEW days were spent busily putting together the pieces of our giant jigsaw puzzle. The dining table wasn't suitable for eating anymore as newspaper clippings, and scribbled notes on yellow legal-size pads covered the surface. Just like old times, we made our way to the large oval coffee table and there among the overflow of data, ate most of our meals.

"This next meeting with Francis is crucial," Charles said as he worked diligently placing events in chronological order.

I watched as Charles made a timeline. He scratched things out, added more items, deleted others, and on and on he went. My head was spinning from all the dates, places, and names.

Francis had agreed to meet us at the same coffee shop as last time.

We were fully prepared this time. Charles had a small tape recorder, and I armed myself with a brand new yellow legal pad. I learned shorthand while in business school and, every so often, it comes in handy.

WE ARRIVED EARLY and found a table where Charles could seat himself facing the door and see Francis when he walked in. I was feeling nervous; the butterflies in my stomach were fluttering away. I felt a small wave of nausea, but after a few sips of water, it passed.

Francis showed up soon after and joined us at our table. He immediately placed a large photo album on the tabletop in front of us. I was hoping it contained pictures of my family and me.

"Thank you for meeting us today, Francis," Charles said.

"Yes, thank you," I added.

He cleared his throat. "This here is a photo album that spans about thirty years or more."

I instinctively reached for the album and carefully opened the cover. I flipped through the pages until I came across one I remembered of Daddy, Teresa and I standing in front of our old car.

"I remember when this was taken," I said excitedly. "Daddy had just bought this car. He was so proud of it. He wanted a picture taken, so Mother obliged him, but she was scowling the whole time."

Charles and Francis let out a chuckle.

"It seems funny now, but then, she never seemed to be happy about anything that involved Daddy—or me for that matter."

I continued to flip pages. But I stopped when one picture caught my eye. Francis realized what I was looking at. "That's," he said pointing, "Teresa, her husband, Eddie, and their son, James."

"Yes, I recognize Teresa. I didn't know Eddie or James. Teresa moved back here to Iowa, and she must've met Eddie then," I said looking up at Francis for acknowledgment.

"Yes, she met Eddie Spencer at a dance hall here in Sioux City."

I went through the rest of the album, but it was mostly people I didn't recognize. I closed the cover and slid it back to Francis. He opened it back up and started naming names, and places of the ones I hadn't known. I had missed a picture of Whitey.

"He was my favorite cousin," I said.

"By the way, we drove out to the nursing home, but Teresa was angry and told us to leave," I told Francis.

"I'm sorry she did that to you. Give her some time," Francis muttered.

"Time? I may not have that much time. We didn't move here to Iowa permanently. We'll only be here a short while longer," I said.

Charles told Francis about our second visit to the farmhouse and how Louise was more forthcoming and had told us about another child of my dad.

"Oh, you mean Thomas," he said matter-of-factly.

I guess I was the only one that didn't know about him. Francis told us he was about four years older than me. I couldn't fathom how they kept him a secret.

"He lived with his mother," Francis replied.

Francis shed light on a new woman in my dad's life, Thomas's mom.

"I knew Teresa was from an earlier relationship of Daddy's but had no idea there were two children."

"It wasn't just a relationship. He was married to Thomas's mother," Francis said.

"Married?" I said, shocked by the news.

Francis nodded, confirming that indeed Lyle, my daddy, had a previous marriage—other than to Teresa's mother. I tried to figure out how that could be. Had he divorced Irma, and then remarried her later? Now things were getting interesting.

"Her name was Mary," Francis told us.

"Mary?" I queried. "Mary as in the initial M that is on the census form we have?" I said shaking.

It turned out that Francis had a wealth of information. More than we could have ever discovered on our own. He gave us names and addresses, he confirmed that Louise was indeed a cousin on my daddy's side, and also that Thomas was indeed my half-brother.

"Why do you suppose Louise didn't want to talk to us at first, but then later opened up?" I asked Francis.

"She's kind of eccentric, that one. I think all the Bowman's were kind of different in one way or another," he said.

"Different?" I asked a bit hurt.

"Well, I don't mean any harm by it, but it's just that they were so good about keeping all the darn secrets—even Lyle, your daddy was good at that. He may have been a good man in your eyes, but he had some part in all of this mess," he spluttered out.

"That's fair enough," I admitted. Taking my cue from Charles that I was getting a bit over-heated, I backed down and let Charles and Francis talk.

"Ok, we now know that Louise is related to Pat and

that she has a half-brother who is now deceased. What can you tell us about Thomas's mother?"

AFTERWARD, we agreed that the meeting with Francis accomplished a lot.

"Louise must know who my mother is then?" I said as we prepared dinner.

"I wouldn't be surprised. It's as if she's been sworn to secrecy over this crap. Maybe if we stumble on the truth, she'll come clean, but in the meantime, we'll have to do all the digging," Charles said as he set the table for dinner.

After dinner, over a glass of wine, we went over the information we'd uncovered thus far. We laid it all out in an organized fashion among the rest of the stuff we'd collected. Charles looked at each piece with an eye of an investigator.

We plotted out our agenda for the following day. We were going to visit the last known address of the mysterious woman who gave birth to Thomas.

CHAPTER 15

ON THE DRIVE to Mary's house, I told Charles that I was getting tired of the circus, and all the running around we were doing just to find out names and associations.

"Don't tell me you want to give up. We've come a long way, and, I think we've done pretty well in uncovering information in the little time we've been here."

"I know you think that, but I know this family, probably better than I realized. They've always been good at keeping secrets, not dealing with issues, and quite frankly, I don't know why I ever felt so compelled to do this."

"I'll tell you why you felt determined to do this. You felt depressed, needed answers, and wanted to find out if you had any blood relations left alive," he said. I felt my face flush. He was right, and I knew it.

"I love you, Charles. You are the best thing that ever happened to me—besides our beautiful children. It seems we're just chasing our tails. I'm sorry for that. I know you don't like to give up or be defeated. I've made up my mind, though. We'll check on these last couple of leads. After that, we're packing it up and going home. Home. I love the sound of that word."

Charles pulled the car over, parked, and pointed to a large gray-stoned house with a wraparound porch. "This must be the house. It's the address Francis gave us as the last known address of Mary."

"This is a very nice neighborhood. I wonder where my dad met this Mary person," I said, taking in the house and the grounds.

"Well, let's get this over with." Charles knocked three times. There was no answer.

"No one must be home," I said and turned to descend the stairs.

Then there was a loud creak, and I turned to see the front door slowly open. There standing in the narrow doorway was an elderly woman with a walker.

I came alongside Charles as he handed the woman one of our business cards.

"Hello, I'm Charles, and this is my wife, Pat. We

were wondering if we could take a few moments of your time. My wife," he explained, nodding my way, "is the daughter of Irma and Lyle Bowman. Did you know them?"

The woman looked me up and down. Then she turned her attention to Charles. She nodded. "I do. I did."

Charles shifted his weight. "Are you Mary?"

She nodded, stepped back, and opened the door wide. Motioning for us to come inside, she said, "I am. Please, come in."

We entered a large formal living room; she seated herself in the center of a beautiful brocade couch and then motioned for us to be seated in a pair of large wingback chairs.

"Would either of you care for some tea?"

Feeling not only comfortable in her home, but also with her kindness, for a moment I hoped that she was my mom.

"Yes, tea would be nice," I said nodding.

"How about you Charles, would you like some tea as well?" Mary asked as she pulled herself up from the couch, grabbing her walker.

Jumping up from my chair, I followed Mary to the kitchen and offered my assistance.

"So," she said looking at us while sipping her tea. "I

don't get many visitors. This is a treat. What can I do for you?"

I didn't know where to start. I wanted to spew out all the questions I had stored in my brain, yet I knew that wouldn't be polite, and could cause her to become tight-lipped. We didn't want that. I did the best thing and looked over to Charles giving him the cue to ask the first few questions.

"As I mentioned, Pat was the daughter of Lyle and Irma Bowman. You must have known them. We're trying to find out some ancestry information. Pat is searching her family tree. We're on an extended vacation gathering data to put together that tree."

I loved how Charles could get people to open up to him. He was the best private investigator in the entire world as far as I was concerned.

Mary put her cup down on the glass top coffee table and cleared her throat. "I did know them. I knew them well." She looked at me long and hard.

I felt a large lump in my throat, and my heart felt like it was going to burst out of my chest.

"It was a long time ago. I was young and very impressionable. I was looking for love, but in all the wrong places, as the song says," she said laughing at her words.

I was starting to feel like I was going to get all my

answers in one fell swoop—here at Mary's house. I inched forward on the couch, eager for the few words I was desperate to hear.

"I met Lyle over at his cousins' house. I was friends with his cousins' younger sister."

Already knowing the answer, I queried, "Which cousin is that?"

"Louise."

Charles and I looked at each other then turned to Mary. "You know we've been to Louise's house, don't you?" I asked her.

She nodded. "I've been waiting for you to come."

I swallowed hard. "Tell us more, please."

"I was seventeen years old and Lyle... well, Lyle was twenty-five and just divorced. He'd been married to Teresa's mom. Anyway, he was sweet, kind, and something about him intrigued me."

"Did you get married?" I blurted out.

"We did. It was a small ceremony. My parents were livid that I was marrying an older man. They disapproved of the marriage. It tore me apart that they didn't want anything to do with me or our son."

"Thomas. My half-brother," I confirmed.

Mary got up from the sofa and retrieved a photo album from a nearby shelf. "The housekeeper isn't doing her job," she said blowing off the dust. "Come and sit over by me. I can tell you more while we look at the photos," she pleaded.

I flipped through the album noticing the age of the pictures. Most of them were black and white.

"This was Thomas when he was about one," and flipping the pages she pointed to another one, "and this was when he was about two."

Pointing to an image of a young couple sprawled on a blanket and looked to be having a picnic, she said, "That's your daddy and me."

"You both look very happy together," I replied.

She nodded. "I loved your daddy. He was the nicest man. I could never understand what he saw in Irma. She was so mean and domineering. In fact, he told me later that Irma was a lot like Teresa's mother, and he couldn't believe he fell for the same type of woman twice."

"What happened to you and Daddy? How did he ever end up with Irma anyway?" I asked.

"Well, that's the twisted part of this whole story."

"One night he was out with his partying cousin, and he ran into Irma. One thing led to another, and he was unfaithful to me. It was just a one-night stand, and it didn't mean anything to him, but I was hurt, and I didn't think I'd ever be able to trust him again. At first, we tried to work it out, but images of Lyle and Irma kept creeping back into my mind. It didn't help that she put the pressure on him as well. She told him if he didn't leave Thomas and me, she'd make his life a living hell. Ours too."

"She was an evil woman, that Irma. So, between me not being able to trust him, and Irma always interfering, we divorced," she murmured.

"Thomas was hurt and never quite forgave Lyle. I forgave him. I knew my heart wouldn't heal and be able to move forward if I didn't forgive him. I guess that's the Christian in me," she told us.

"I don't know if I could have been so forgiving. I truthfully didn't know Daddy could be capable of anything so distasteful either. I guess, in my eyes, he was always the hero, and nothing Irma did was right. I'm not sure if I should feel sorry for Daddy and the miserable life he had with her."

"Don't be so hard on him, dear. It was so long ago."

"When Irma and Lyle moved to California, I was relieved. I wouldn't have to see him, or her for that matter and ..."

"And?"

"And you."

"Who is my mother?" I blurted out.

"I don't know," she said getting comfortable on the couch.

"Well, we have an old census sheet showing Irma with a child at the Mt. Saint Francis convent. You wouldn't be that M. Brown, would you?" The investigative side of me asked.

"If you're trying to connect me with her, don't bother," she said disgustedly. "I'm not related to her in any way, shape or form. The "M" you refer to is for Irma. Her real name was Mary Irma. Folks around here just called her Irma."

Stunned with the new information, I looked to Charles. "M. Brown was Irma. What about the P. Brown that was with her?" I asked.

"Well. I don't know for certain, but I'm betting it was her little pain in the butt sister, Priscilla Inez. But she was called Inez around here."

"When was the last time you saw Teresa?" I boldly asked.

"Oh, it's been years. However, this is a small town, so back in the day, we'd run into each other now and then. We didn't hate each other; we just didn't respect one another."

"Oh, why is that?" I asked.

"Well, she always saw any woman that came into Lyle's life as someone who had the potential to steal his love for her. She had some issues for sure. She was a bratty child, and from what I've been told, and, even more, hostile adult. Irma was the only one who could keep her in line. I think she was afraid of her."

"I bet. I was scared of Irma too." I exclaimed. "Teresa was mean to me. She'd slap me, push me down in the dirt, and pull my hair. I bet these were all learned traits, from Irma," I added.

"Lyle did the best he could. But as you know, he was a man of few words. He probably gave up on her. But boy was he protective of you," she chuckled.

I paused a moment, taking in everything Mary was telling us. My throat felt dry, and I cleared my throat. "We went out to the nursing home to see Teresa. She wasn't very receptive to our visit. She told us to leave. I think we should make another visit out there. Maybe this time, I can get her to talk."

"What more do you want to know?" Mary said cocking her head.

"I don't know. I guess I'd like to ask her one more time if she knew who my real mother was."

Shaking her head, she said, "You'll just be setting yourself up for more heartbreak. Let sleeping dogs lie," she added.

Changing the subject, I asked, "How did Thomas die?"

Mary looked past us and gazed out the large picture window. I could see a small tear forming in her eye. After all these years the memory was still painful. "That was such an awful time for me, and for Elaine. They'd only been married a year when the accident happened. He was on a ladder to get up on the roof of their new house. He was going to do some repair work. The ladder slipped, and he fell 25 feet, hitting his head on a rock as he landed. He died instantly."

I reached out and gently touched her hand. "I'm so sorry."

"He was my only child," she quietly said.

The room went suddenly quiet. A moment of silence seemed appropriate.

"One last question, and then we'll get out of your hair. Why has Louise been so secretive about things? What does she have to gain?" I asked.

"Louise always has been ... well ... strange. I think she's lived in the country too long," she added laughing.

I nodded. I was aware of all the game playing this family could do, but I was always surprised by the next level of game playing we came across.

"Well, we've probably taken up too much of your time this afternoon. It was a pleasure meeting you. I can see what Lyle loved about you. You seem like a very sweet woman."

"Well dear, it's nice seeing you again. You're all

grown up now. Do you have children of your own?" She asked.

"Oh yes. We have three children. Charlie, Carole, and Peter."

"Grandchildren?" She asked.

"Yes, we have a few," I smiled thinking of them as I dug in my purse for the pictures.

After a few moments of showing off the children and grandchildren, I hugged Mary good-bye, and Charles and I left the big stone home on the tree-lined street.

We sat in the car staring out onto the street. I looked at each house with an investigative eye. I looked intently at every window, every shrub, and every small detail I could focus on. Charles knew my wheels were turning.

"You heard what Mary said. Let sleeping dogs lie," Charles said.

"I know. I just want one more try with Teresa. She is my sister," I reminded him.

He reached over and kissed me on the nose. He leaned back into the seat and sighed. "Are you sure?" he said turning toward me.

I nodded. "I'm sure. This is my last opportunity."

"You wait in the car," I ordered when we pulled up to the nursing home.

Looking rather shocked, but nevertheless obedient, Charles stayed in the car.

When I found Teresa's room, she was reading a book.

"Oh, so you enjoy literary works, do you?" I sneered.

"What are you doing here?" She smirked back.

"Listen. You can hate me if that's what you want. Me? I prefer not to hate. It takes too much energy, and I don't have time for it. I've met a lot of friendly and interesting folks this time in Iowa," I said pulling up a chair.

"Well, I'm glad. But, like I told you, Lyle and Irma were your parents, and as much as I hate admitting it, Daddy loved you more than me." Then she added in a whisper, "That's always bothered me."

Feeling somewhat sad that she'd always felt this way, I softly said, "He did not love me more. I was little, and you were a pain in the butt teenager. He just wanted me to have every opportunity for love and acceptance, which I'm sure you had too."

"My mother was not that kind; especially after Lyle— she and Daddy divorced. I went to live with Irma and Daddy, and that got under Mother's collar."

I nodded. I knew how that felt. "I don't want to rehash that old stuff. I just have a couple of questions. You insist that Lyle and Irma were my biological parents. Ok, I can't prove otherwise, but what about Thomas? Why did you disown him too?"

"I was hurt. I wanted Daddy all to myself. It just propelled me into hate and eventually, I didn't like anyone or anything. Heck, I didn't even like Irma," she confided.

"She was a hard one to like," I agreed.

"Anyway, Thomas is dead, Daddy is gone, and so is Irma," Teresa said.

I nodded. I wanted to stay focused on my line of questioning. I locked eyes with Teresa. "What about Priscilla? Did you know about her?

"Priscilla? I don't know anyone by that name."

"She was better known around here as Inez."

CHAPTER 16

"HOW'D IT GO?" Charles asked as he started up the car.

"Just as I expected. At least, she didn't throw anything at me," I laughed.

"Did you find out anything?"

"Yes. She said she knew Inez."

Tilting his head toward me, he said, "Oh, do tell me more."

"She confirmed that she is still alive. She said for me to ask Francis the details. She didn't want to get involved anymore. She said too many years had passed and that I should just go about my business."

He took my hand, held it firmly and said, "We mustn't give up. We're close. I can feel it." Nodding my head, I agreed. "What's next on the agenda?"

"Well, I think we should meet with Louise again. After all, she was the one who introduced Mary to your daddy. And now we have confirmation of Inez from both Mary and Teresa. Besides, I'm curious what other curveballs she'll throw at us," he said amused.

We didn't bother to call her, just showed up on the stoop. After all, we were family. Louise opened the door and invited us in.

Motioning for us to have a seat at the table, Louise went straight to the cupboard to get cups for coffee. As she prepared our drinks, she talked from the kitchen, raising her voice slightly.

"Mary called. I'm glad you went and talked to her. She's a great lady. I know your daddy loved her to pieces, Pat. I've been told they were the cutest couple despite the age difference. And, Thomas, well, he was the most adorable little guy. He turned all the girls' heads here in town. He ended up marrying Elaine."

"Yes, Mary told us about Elaine. Do you know her last name?"

"Elaine Panelli. A local girl. Her parents owned the meat market."

"The meat market," I echoed. "The one around the corner from the pool hall and apartment we lived in?"

"Yes, that one."

"I just had a flashback of Daddy giving me a

quarter and telling me to walk to the meat market and get three pork chops. The butcher would select three meaty ones, wrap them in paper and tie it up with string."

"They had the freshest meat," Louise said. "Anyway, your daddy loved Mary with all his heart. What that bitch Irma did to him was evil. Plain, simple evil."

"Well, maybe so, but he did cheat on Mary," I said. "You reap what you sow," I added.

"Cheat on Mary? Did Mary tell you that?"

Looking puzzled, I nodded my head slowly. My brain quickly checked to see if maybe I had heard Mary wrong. But wait, no, I couldn't have. Charles was with me. He must have heard the same thing. I looked at Charles, and he nodded.

"Yes. Mary told us that Daddy messed around with Irma, and she held it over his head. He divorced Mary so that they could live in peace."

"After all, this time, I thought Mary knew the truth. We never speak of it. In fact, you coming here to Iowa is making all this stuff resurface. Stuff we'd just as soon forget about. Lyle didn't cheat on Mary. Lyle got drunk, and Irma made him think something happened between them. That's the only way she could ever get a man. She was mean and not the most attractive woman, so she had to stoop to a new low to get a man."

"What? He didn't cheat on Mary. Irma tricked him? That makes total sense to me. I knew he couldn't have done that to Mary. Louise, you need to contact Mary and tell her the truth. You've not been a good friend letting her think the worst about Lyle all these years. Why are you all so hell-bent on keeping these dirty little secrets alive, especially ones that aren't even true?" I said in a sharp tone.

Suddenly I grew a backbone. I was tired. Fed up. The lies, the distortions, had to stop. Charles leaned back and observed. He lightly chuckled. This was a different side of me.

"I'll give you to the end of the week to tell Mary the truth. I'll be checking in on her before we leave,"

Louise lowered her head. "I feel awful for not telling her the truth. It just seems around every corner something has to be clarified, apologized for, and well—"

I cut her off. "Is Mary my mother?" I asked pointedly.

"Oh no, dear. She's not. We don't know who your mother was. Lyle always said you were discovered inside their house after returning from church."

I shook my head, "I can't believe there isn't one living person in this whole darn town who knows the truth about my birth. I didn't just drop from the sky. I am someone's child. I have a biological mother and father, and it doesn't make sense, after all these years, to still keep who they are a secret."

Charles broke in, "Listen, Louise, Pat doesn't mean any harm. She's feeling a bit frustrated with the turn of events. She finds out that Lyle has been married more than twice, and she finds out she has not only a half-sister but a half-brother. You can imagine her disappointment in not finding out the information that was the main reason for our visit here in Iowa, the name of her biological mother and/or father," he said.

"I understand completely. I really do. All I can tell you is that Lyle announced to us that they found you in their home. I will say that the stories that have been handed down always cast suspicion on the story of you, but no one could ever prove it. Family stories passed down always painted you as an adorable child."

I pushed back my chair and stood up.

"Thanks, Louise. I'm exhausted by today's events. Heck, I'm exhausted period. We'll talk again before we leave town."

"Leave town? Are you ..." She stammered.

"Yes, we only came to get answers. We didn't get what we came for. It's time for us to head home," I said.

In a last-ditch effort to pull any more information

from Louise, I blurted out, "Did you know Irma's sister?"

Louise frowned. "Yes, Inez. Irma raised her. She went off to Texas to be with the Brown family. She came to visit once in a while. I don't think they had the best relationship. They were several years apart. I think Irma saw her as more of a burden."

"That's ironic. She thought of me as a burden too," I added.

"So not only did you know the Bowman's, you knew the Brown's as well," I said giving her the look of disapproval.

"Guilty as charged," she said, her face flushing.

"Remember what I told you. You make it right with Mary, or else."

Looking down at her feet, Louise said in nearly a whisper, "I will dear, I promise."

Louise walked us to the door. It was a quiet walk. No one had anything else to say. As we drove away, I saw her looking out the battered screen door. She looked as if her best friend was leaving, never to return.

ARRIVING BACK AT OUR BUNGALOW, I walked straight into the kitchen and poured myself a glass of wine. I didn't usually drink before eating, but this had been one of the days I made an exception.

I opened up cabinets to find something to prepare for dinner. I wasn't really in the mood to cook, but I decided to make a tuna casserole anyway. I gathered all the stuff needed to make it, and I guess I made a bit too much noise as Charles came into the kitchen and asked me if everything was ok.

"I heard cabinet doors slamming and pots clanging. Can I help?"

I broke down right there in the kitchen. "It's so unfair," I cried.

"Listen, Pat, I told you this wouldn't be easy. If you're ready to go back home, let's do it. No harm done. We turned over a few rocks and found out a few interesting facts. I was hoping for more, but ... What do you say? Shall we head home?" He said hugging me and wiping my tears away with his hand.

In between sobs, I said, "We've come so far. Let's see it through to the end."

Charles hugged me tighter. "That's my girl," he whispered.

CHAPTER 17

WITH RENEWED VIGOR, I reviewed the new information. Daddy hadn't cheated on Mary. All, this time, she'd thought he had. Why in the world did she think that, and moreover, how were they able to convince her he had? Even more importantly, how in the heck did Irma convince Lyle that he had? That was a new puzzle for me to put together.

Charles and I needed to meet with Francis again. We were convinced he'd give us the final information we needed to conclude our visit. He knew so much about my family and little oddities that only family or close friends would know. Charles arranged for a meeting for the following day.

The next day, I paced the room clenching my

hands until it was time to go. "Is it time yet?" I said looking at my watch once again.

Charles sighed and got up from the sofa. "Not yet, but let's go anyway. We'll just be early, drink some coffee and have some pie."

"THANKS FOR MEETING US TODAY, FRANCIS," I said as I considered how I was going to approach the subject with him.

I witnessed him squirm a bit in his seat, and a bead of sweat appeared on his brow. He started rapping his fingers on the table. "Is everything alright?" I asked him, staring him down, hoping I would break him down as well.

He nodded. "I'm good," he said.

Charles started the conversation. "A few things have happened since we last spoke. We met with Mary. She was very nice."

"Yeah, she's a sweetheart," Francis agreed.

Charles responded, "We've met with Louise again. She spilled the beans. Lyle hadn't cheated on Mary as everyone was led to believe."

Shaking his head, Charles tapped his fingers on the table and continued, "I don't understand how Lyle could have been so naïve to think he'd been unfaithful to Mary with Irma."

Francis clenched his jaw. "Well, you didn't know Irma," Francis replied. "She was something else. Her family was part of a gypsy clan that had settled in the area. They'd originally come from Texas, and she had all kinds of tricks up her sleeves. That's how she survived on the streets."

"A Gypsy Clan?" I asked louder than I had intended.

"Yep, she found her way here as a teenager and brought her little sister with her. That's how they ended up in that convent."

"Are you saying that Irma and Inez both were at the convent as youngsters?" I blurted out.

"Irma and Inez also known as Mary and Priscilla left Texas and came to Iowa because they had family here. Once they arrived here in Iowa, that family wouldn't help them, so Irma did what she could, and sought help at the convent."

"What about Irma's sister? Do you have any information about her?" Charles asked.

"I know that she lived most of the time in Texas after she turned eighteen. She occasionally came here to visit. Their relationship was volatile, so she didn't stay long. Irma always thought she was after Lyle."

Charles and I looked at each other. "Do you think that Inez could be my mother?"

"Rumor had it she was in town for a few days before the news was leaked out to the police and press that you had been discovered in their house," Francis revealed.

Charles and I exchanged looks of surprise, but also of relief. We may have hit on something, finally.

"Do you have an address for Inez in Texas?" I asked.

"She doesn't live in Texas anymore. She moved back here not long ago," Francis added.

With a surprised look on my face, I searched his face for more clues. "Do you have her address here," I asked.

WE DROVE in silence to the address that Francis gave us. It was only a few blocks away from Mary's home. We walked up to the door and knocked a few times. A woman, dressed in casual clothes answered.

"How can I help you?

"My name is Patricia Bowman-Phillips. Does an Inez Brown live here?

"Inez does live here, but her last name is Ramos.

Her maiden name was Brown, however," she added.

The woman invited us in. "Please, sit down," she said gesturing to the couch. "How do you know Inez?"

"Well, that's the million-dollar question. I could be her daughter," I blurted out.

"Patsy?" She asked smiling

I gasped, "Yes. How'd you know that?"

"I know all about you. Inez has dementia and will not remember you at all. But up until about three or four years ago, she told me the story of her and Lyle ... and you, all the time. She loved you a lot, but she was very young, and, unfortunately, didn't make right decisions regarding you."

My heart was suddenly filled with both joy and apprehension. "What else do you know?" I asked.

"I know that Inez and Irma were sisters and that Irma and Lyle raised you. But, it was too hard on Inez to see you all the time, so she moved back to Texas. She got married but never had any other children."

"I see," I whispered.

"Her husband was a wealthy oilman, and she has been set up for life in this charming home," she said taking in the room's grandeur.

Not knowing how to respond, I just answered, "That's great for her."

"Would you like to see her?"

I looked at Charles. He nodded for me to go.

"Charles, come with me," I pleaded.

The woman led us to a room down a hallway. As we approached the room, I saw a frail, gray-haired woman sitting in a wheelchair gazing out a huge picture window.

"You have visitors, Inez," the lady said.

She didn't respond. I didn't expect her to, and honestly, the caregiver didn't either. It was just about pleasantries and respect.

The caregiver moved the wheelchair around so we could see her face. This was my mother. The mother I never knew. I choked back the tears. It was so surreal. After all these years, after all, the questions, the memories, I had now come face to face with the woman I'd been searching my whole life for.

I stood frozen for a few seconds. What would I say to this woman I didn't know. What was I expecting? She had a major illness that wouldn't allow her to recall anything. What did I think I was going to get from her? After a few more seconds, I began to speak.

"Inez, it's me, Patsy ... Patsy, your daughter."

Nothing. No facial expression, no tears forming in her eyes, no twitching, nothing.

I tried one more time. I reached out and gently caressed her hand. Her hands were cool to the touch.

"Inez, my name is Patsy Bowman. Lyle was my father. I came to say hello. We finally get to meet," I added, desperate for some sign of recognition.

A mumble came out of her mouth. No one could make out what she said, but undoubtedly, she was trying, to say something.

"I think she understands you," the caregiver said.

I tried one last time. I'd come all this way. I just had to know if she knew it was me, Patsy, her long last daughter standing before her. This was the day that both of us only ever dreamed could happen.

Pulling up a chair, I sat right in front of her. I took both her hands and gently massaged them.

"Inez, this is my husband, Charles. He's the love of my life. We have three children. They're your grandchildren. Charles Jr., Carole, and Peter."

I paused for a moment, took a deep breath, and then tried again.

"We live in California. We have a small business there, and we like it a lot," I said looking up at the two people in the room with me for guidance.

"Well, I can see you are well taken care of. I don't harbor any bad feelings toward you. You were young, and you did what you did. Daddy played as much of a part in it as you did. Irma was in the middle. She had to live with the fact that Daddy betrayed her, and I was a constant reminder that he hadn't been faithful. I wish you well, Inez... Mother."

I got up and gently touched her shoulder. "God Bless you, Mom," I said.

"Patsy."

I gasped and turned around to face Inez. She'd said my name. "Yes, it's me. Patsy," I said anxiously.

But, there was nothing. Not another word came out of her mouth. She closed her eyes and drifted off to sleep.

"She nods off a lot during the day," the caregiver said.

I slumped back into the chair, feeling disappointed, but also realizing there was nothing more to gain from our visit. I reached over, caressed her hand and said, "Good-bye, Mom. I love you."

I slowly stood and said, "Well, I suppose we should be going. Thanks so much for letting us see her."

"It was my pleasure. I'm so glad you got to see her at least. I know she didn't make all the right decisions as a young woman, but she tried to make up for it. She was very active in donating to the orphanages, and she sponsored a few foster children as well. She always thought of you, but she also thought it best not to inter-fere with your life. It may not have been the right deci-sion, but it was hers nevertheless."

WE PACKED up all our belongings. I'd done a thorough cleaning of the apartment, making sure that we'd get our deposit back. Charles packed all the suitcases in the carrier attached to the roof of our car. A couple of large plastic containers which held household items filled the back cargo area of our vehicle. I made a nice bed for Spunky so he'd be comfortable as we made the long trek back to California.

"Everything is all packed. Let's do one last walkthrough of the house to make sure we didn't leave anything behind," I said, delaying our departure some.

Charles was on to me. He knew me well. I had a hard time with departures.

After I convinced myself the house was clear of all

our belongings, we walked out the door, locking it behind us.

We drove for a few minutes, stopping in front of the real estate office that leased us the house.

"I'll be right back," Charles announced.

Spunky and I sat in the car listening to the radio, waiting for Charles. My mind was blank. I was exhausted beyond anything I'd ever felt before. I was ready to go home and see the family and neighbors.

WE DECIDED we were going to try and locate Teresa's son. We'd found out he was living in Corpus Christi, Texas. It was a little out of our way, but at least, we'd get to see that part of the gulf coast. Corpus Christi was a vacation destination for many families because of their beaches.

We found a place to stay for the night, and then Charles looked up the address for his law firm. He thought it might be simpler to make an unannounced visit. It always scared me to do these, but Charles always said it was the best way.

THE OFFICE WAS A SINGLE STORY, wood framed building. The exterior was battered; no doubt from the severe weather Corpus Christie endured each year during hurricane season.

We entered the building and saw a small counter with a woman sitting behind it was to our immediate right.

"Can I help you?" The woman politely asked.

"Yes, you can. We'd like to see James Spencer."

She replied, "Do you have an appointment?"

Charles responded, "No, we don't. Please tell him Charles and Pat Phillips are here." Spunky let out a little bark letting the lady know he was there too. She peered over her desk to see him.

"He's a good dog. He won't cause any trouble. I didn't want to leave him in the car," I said.

The young woman pushed her chair out from behind the desk and walked down a hallway to another room. We could hear conversations in the offices we passed. Our footsteps echoed loudly as we walked down the wooden floored hallway.

Opened a door toward the end of the hallway and escorted us into a little anteroom. At the same time, the inner door opened. There standing in the door was a man we assumed was James.

"Please, follow me," he said as he gestured for us to come.

I already knew I'd let Charles do most of the talking. We already found out everything about the adoption and the cover-up. We just wanted to introduce ourselves.

Charles looked over at me. I nodded for him to take the lead. "My name is Charles Phillips, and this is my wife, Pat."

James acknowledged our greeting by nodding his head.

Motioning for us to have a seat, James sat behind the large wooden desk and waited for us to continue.

I cleared my throat and began. "I was known as Patsy when a child. Maybe that name sounds familiar?"

James' eyes widened. He started to act restless and began thumping his fingers on the top of his desk. "Go on," he said.

"Your mother, Teresa, is my half sister."

James smiled. "I guess we're related then."

I nodded. "We just are on our way back home to California, and thought we'd stop by and introduce ourselves," I said.

The corners of James' mouth turned up. He

brushed his hand across his face. "I guess you came to find out answers. Did you find them?" He asked.

I responded, "Yes. It's been quite the trip."

He nodded his head. "I'm glad the trip was fulfilling then."

"We won't keep you any longer, but just wanted to say hi, and if you ever take a trip our way, please stop by. We have three children, and grandchildren that would accept you with open arms," I said with a small tear trailing down my cheek.

"That's good, Pat. I'm happy to hear that. I won't pretend to know how it feels or be able to offer you any advice. But, I'm glad you found out the truth, though," he said.

"Just because your mother and I didn't have the best relationship doesn't mean we can't. I promise I will never try to turn you away from your mom. She loves you, and I'm sure you love her. If you want a relationship with me, then that would be fine too."

"Thanks for the offer. I'll consider that."

He walked out from his desk and extended his hand to Charles. He then came over to me and gave me a gentle hug. He reached down and gave Spunky a pat on the head. We'd said what we came to say. Now we could continue on home.

Charles and I didn't say too much about our visit with James. Instead, we went down to the beach and walked barefoot in the sand along the water, and let Spunky enjoy some freedom. He'd been so good about being in the car for hours on end. We ended our visit to the beach with fried clams and fries from a nearby fish shack.

AFTER FIVE, long days on the road, we pulled up in our driveway. It was so good to be home. I rushed to the front door where Peter and Charlie were waiting for us.

After hugging and kissing them both a multitude of times, I asked them where the rest of the crowd was.

"They'll be calling you over the next few days. They wanted to give you time to settle back into your routine," Charlie said smiling.

Charles brought in all the suitcases and greeted the kids as he struggled with the luggage.

"A little help here, please," he said.

"I'm sorry, dear. I was so happy to see the kids," I said taking one of the bags from him.

"Well, Mom and Dad, you must be tired. We can catch up tomorrow. We just wanted to be here to say welcome back."

"We love you guys," I yelled as they walked out the door.

"We have the best kids," I said to Charles.

He nodded. "When are you going to tell them?" He asked.

"I'm going to invite them all over for dinner. We'll tell them together," I said in between yawns.

We both slept like babies, and even Spunky was sawing logs in his cushy bed. Being home was great.

OVER THE COURSE of the next few days, Charles and I got back into our routine. We ate a light breakfast, went for a long walk, taking Spunky with us. We'd come back to the house and do a few chores, and then have lunch. Charles still did some investigating part time. But he even had to admit, he needed some time off after our trip to Iowa.

I called each of the kids and invited them and their families to dinner. We set the date for a week from Sunday. The only ones that would be missing from the group would be Carole and her family.

Charles and I planned the menu. We both enjoyed cooking as much as we liked to eat. We decided on grilled steaks, baked potatoes, corn on the cob, and for dessert, strawberry shortcake. It was near the end of summer, and we wanted to get in one last barbecue before summer was over—although summer was almost year-round in California.

THE KIDS ARRIVED ON TIME, and we sat outside talking and sipping wine. It was so good to see Charles and our sons laughing and talking sports. I had missed my family so much while we were away.

Peter tossed a Frisbee out for Spunky to fetch. Charles grilled the steaks to perfection. We sat around the patio table eating and enjoying one another's company.

"Mom, are you going to tell us what you found out in Iowa?" Peter asked.

I could see all the kids looking at me, waiting for me to come clean.

"Yes, I was just waiting for the right time."

I told them everything. I told them how we met Francis, and Louise, and Mary. I told the kids how Francis had so much information and Louise was a distant relative and Mary. I told the kids poor Mary's story too.

I cleared my throat, and I looked to Charles. He nodded at me assuring me he had my back.

I pulled out the picture I had of a teenager with a young child. It was the one from the convent. I told the children that the teen was Irma, and the little girl was her sister, Inez. I could see the shocked look on their faces. A new name added to the mix.

"Inez?" Peter answered.

"Priscilla Inez is her full name. You see, Inez is my mother."

All at once you could hear the surprised sounds coming from each of their mouths.

"Not only did I find out who my biological mother was, but I also found out who my real dad was too. Lyle was married to his first wife, and they had Teresa. The marriage ended in divorce, and that's when he fell in love with Mary and had my half-brother, Thomas. During a visit to a bar one night, Lyle ran into both Irma and her sister Inez. Inez apparently had been eyeing Daddy, and the two of them came up with getting him drunk. Dad did love his whiskey. Anyway, he got drunk and passed out. Irma came up with the story that he had messed around with her, and that is what caused the breakup of Mary's and Lyle's marriage." I took a drink of my wine. My throat was getting dry, but I could see all eyes on me, wanting me to finish the story.

"So, Irma goes in for the kill, and one thing led to another and Irma and Lyle are married. Daddy is never happy with her, and he starts to do what he'd been accused of all along. He cheats on his wife. He ends up getting Inez pregnant. Irma is angry, and so they come up with the harebrained idea of someone leaving me on the bed in their house."

"Oh, Mom, that's crazy. I mean what the heck were those people drinking?" Charles Jr. asked.

"It was the depression. People did all kinds of crazy things. I'm just glad to find out that Lyle was, in fact, my real dad. That was so important to me. I loved him, and I could feel his love to the very end."

"What about Inez? Is she still alive?" Charles Jr. asked.

I gathered my strength for the last part of the story.

"Yes, she's seventy-five years old and has severe dementia. She didn't know who I was, but a nurse who had worked there for several years knew about me and filled Dad and me in on all the details. You see, my dad cared about Inez. The problem was she was young and didn't want to settle down. She lived in Texas but would come to Iowa now and then, and stir up trouble.

She and Irma did not have the best of relationships. Irma saw her as a burden."

"We're so sorry, Mom. I know you wanted to get to know her," Peter said.

"I did know her—somewhat. After everyone had come clean, I recalled several times a lady would come visit me. She'd bring me toys, and play games with me. Irma was not nice to her, though. I remember that as well. After we moved to California, I never saw her again."

"Why do you think it was so imperative that everyone keep that secret from you, Mom?" Peter asked.

"Yeah, Mom," Charlie echoed.

"I guess to cover up embarrassment and shame. Who knows? If Irma told the truth, then everyone would have known Lyle was a cheater. It would have made him look bad. Maybe she did have some love for him after all. She did protect him, I guess."

"Are you okay with what you know?" Peter asked.

"I'm more than okay. I have a wonderful husband, three great children, who all married incredible people. I also have the best grandchildren a woman could ask for," I said smiling at each of them. "My cup runneth over," I said with a tear in my eye.

I looked around the table and saw all the twinkling

eyes and bright smiles. At that very moment, something so profound hit me. I had the best family right here. I didn't need to travel clear across the United States to discover that. Those days in Iowa were in the past. It's true, the past made me who I was today, but it wouldn't determine my whole legacy or my path to happiness.

It had been difficult for me as a young mother to understand how a mother could be so mean to their child. I guess that is essentially what drove me to investigate my adoption.

I should have listened to Charles. He said it didn't matter. It was only important how I lived my life today. As usual, he was right.

EPILOGUE

THE YEARS ROLLED by and with each passing one, Charles and I got older. Unfortunately, with age comes not just wisdom, but aches and pains and if you're unlucky, doctor appointments. It seems to happen suddenly. One day we were young and carefree, and the next we were shrouded with doctor appointments, surgery dates, and hospital stays.

I didn't want to focus on the negative, but deep down inside I knew the end was coming. The doctors said things like bad heart, and liver, kidneys failing, and it would just be a matter of time before I'd lose my beloved Charles.

I shouldn't have been surprised that his declining health would lead to death. But how can anyone truly prepare for the death of a loved one, especially their loving husband?

After Charles passed, I found it difficult to cope. He'd been my rock for so many years. My spirits were lifted when Carole told me the good news that they'd be moving back to California to be near me. If it weren't for my children, I'd have been very lonely.

Carole and I spent many delightful afternoons together. She was great about going with me on senior trips, and Saturday shopping and lunches. I looked forward to spending time with all of my children. The boys and their families were wonderful too. I don't know what I would have done without them.

My own health started showing signs of decline. First, I was diagnosed with heart problems, and then rheumatoid arthritis, which caused me severe pain, and the last big blow, a broken hip after someone opened a door into a hallway and knocked me over—walker and all. But, I still tried to live life to the full, and no matter what obstacles were put in my path, I found a way to maneuver around them. My strength now came from my incredible children.

I'd learned to be independent at a very young age, and it served me well in my older years. I didn't want to bother the children. They had their own lives to lead. But, I also knew that with my health issues and not being a licensed driver, I'd have to bother them with my frequent doctor visits. It worried that they'd think I was a nuisance. Instead of being annoyed, they always made me feel loved.

DOCTOR APPOINTMENTS, hospital stays, and emergency room visits became the norm for me. Soon, I would require full-time care. The doctor talked to the children and me about hospice. At first, I thought it meant death was immediate—like tomorrow. I wasn't ready to check out yet. I had a lot of living to do, and I told him as much. Our granddaughter was going to have a baby; my great grandson and I planned to be around to meet him.

They told me that hospice wasn't about giving up hope; it was about making me comfortable.

"You'll go back to your apartment, and you'll live each day to the best of your ability," the kids said.

It was quite an experience, this hospice set up. The first few days new furniture and equipment were brought in, medicine trays filled, and doctors taking my blood pressure and all the other vitals. Everyone was so nice. It lifted my spirits to be surrounded by so many caring individuals. It takes a special person to be a caregiver.

Hospice, assisted living, and caregivers were now part of my life. It was an adjustment, but what are you going to do when you're eighty-six years old and dependent on others? That was the hardest part for me. To be dependent on others. Something I swore would never happen. It was out of my hands, now.

After all the commotion had settled down, I began to get into a routine. I had my favorite caregivers, and they became like family to me. The kids were comforted by knowing how well they treated me, and how well I liked them. After all, you don't just want anyone taking care of your loved one.

The kids would sometimes pop in unannounced, and it made me happy to know they cared so much. It was a different feeling we shared from the one I had with my own mother.

Soon after, I graduated to a wheelchair full-time. I gave up any hope of walking again. I knew that if I didn't move, or stay active, I'd only shorten my life. But, I was eighty-six years old and tired, so I decided to give in to the wheelchair and just be happy with what I could do.

Carole and the other children were always positive. They knew that my days were numbered, but they never gave up hope. Carole was always planning something for us to do. She'd look at the activities calendar, and we'd plan accordingly.

After a while, I didn't really care about the activities. The one thing I looked forward to every day was going outside. The caregivers and Carole would take me out, and we'd enjoy the fresh air and sunshine as we talked and laughed. Soon, I got the boys in on the walks, too.

I knew what the children were going through had to be difficult. They were trying to hold down jobs, take care of their family, and take care of me. I was thankful for everything they did, but I probably didn't voice it enough. However, I was doing everything I could just to hold on. It was harder than I expected.

I wasn't ready to check out of this life yet, but I knew that God would make that decision when it was time. I was a spiritual person, and I believed for every season there was a reason, and for every life, there was another life beyond Earth. If I didn't believe that, then I would never see any of my family again. That would be more painful than anything I'd suffered from deteriorating discs, surgeries, and infections.

It was an unusually warm early spring day, and Carole called to say she was coming over. She had something to share with me. I was always excited to see her. She came bouncing in with a huge grin. She quickly sat next to me on the sofa and handed me a book. She knew my eyesight would not allow me to read anymore.

"Mom. This is our finished project. I finished *your* story," she said gleaming.

I ran my hand over the glossy cover. "Hand me my magnifying glass," I said.

I checked out the front cover intently. It was beautiful. My daughter's name was displayed proudly on the bottom. I turned the book over. "Hummingbird," I said.

Carole nodded. A tear formed on the bottom of her eyelid, mine too. "You remembered how much I love them. I miss seeing them flap their little wings at the feeder. I used to watch them for hours out the kitchen window."

I flipped through the pages. The smell of the paper and print made my heart swell. "Will you read it to me?" I asked.

"Of course, mom. Every day I'll read a little to you," Carole said, her voice a bit choked with emotion.

I COULD SEE and feel a difference in my body. It was changing. I didn't want to alarm the kids, but things were happening, and they were happening faster than I wanted. I wasn't ready to throw in the towel. I guess I saw it as a sign of weakness. I never wanted the children to think I'd given up when they'd done nothing of the sort.

I insisted every day on doing my regular daily routine. Get up, get dressed—even if it was just a clean nightgown, eat a little breakfast, take a few sips of my coffee, and brush my teeth and hair. Then I'd sit on the couch for hours dozing, and perking up only when I was asked if I wanted to go outside.

I loved being outside. I could breathe easier—get rid of that darn oxygen tank, and loved seeing the green and flowers everywhere.

I loved the weekends because I'd usually see each one of my children. They'd take turns and push my wheelchair outside, we'd sip on cold water while lounging outside, and we'd always check out what was going on in the activities room.

It was becoming more challenging to get around the apartment. Most of my days were spent sitting on the couch, using the restroom, and my outings outside or down to the music center. Carole was worried I was getting depressed. I was. I didn't share that with her, though. They were doing everything they could to help me. But there was no way I was going to burden them with the added complication of my depression.

CAROLE CAME BOUNCING into the apartment one afternoon with a hummingbird feeder, a wind chime that was an angel, and a couple of hanging baskets of colorful flowers.

"What's all of this?" I inquired.

"I'm going to make your balcony beautiful," she said getting to work hanging baskets. "Dad's rose bush is lonely out there."

"Ah. Dad's rose bush," I said recalling how she and I went to the gravesite and Carole took a clipping of the rose bush that was planted there. She nursed it, and now it was thriving. I admired it every day, and the caregivers would clip a rose every few days, and put it in a bud vase on the table near me so that I could appreciate it.

When she was done, my balcony was transformed from bland to one that had colorful hanging baskets, a hummingbird feeder, and a wind chime. She'd thought of everything. I thoroughly enjoyed looking out the patio now, and believe it or not, hummingbirds came all the time.

One afternoon the caregiver went outside to water the plants and came right back in saying, "Pat, you're not going to believe this."

"What is it?"

"In the pot with your husband's rose bush are three four-leaf clovers growing."

"You're kidding," I said shocked.

She quickly got me in my wheelchair out and wheeled me out to see. There, growing in the pot, just like she'd said were three four-leaf clovers. I took it as a sign.

THURSDAY WAS a rough day for me. I woke up crying, and upset. It was something the caregivers had never seen before. I tried very hard to be strong for everyone concerned.

On Saturday, I woke up crying again. The caretaker helped me out of bed. I felt different. I'd been having a bad couple of days and wondered if this was the end.

"What day is it?"

The caregiver confirmed it was Saturday. I'd see the kids today. I knew when they came I wouldn't alarm them by telling them how I felt. I'd just let God and nature take its course, but I felt this was the day I was going to be with their dad. It was the day the angels would sing, and carry me off to a world free of pain and disappointment. I knew it would be a sad day for them, but I was ready.

Carole came over to see me. I was not feeling well, but I knew she was there. We talked a little in and out of my drowsiness and hallucinations. I still managed to crack a few jokes, trying to make her feel better. I could see it in her eyes, hear it in her voice, she knew if it weren't today, it would be soon.

She knelt down on the floor and took my hand in hers.

"Mom, what's going on? Do you feel ok?"

"No, I'm hurting. I'm in pain. I'm hurting just like when my ribs were broken."

She squeezed my hand. I opened my eyes and looked at her. The expression on her face told me I didn't look too well, and I might be alarming her, but I didn't want to lie to her.

"I'm tired of fighting; I'm tired of always being in pain."

"Mom, you don't have to fight anymore. It's ok, you

gave it your all," she said, her voice cracking with emotion. "You are one of the strongest women I've ever known. You can go be with Dad now."

I heard her tell my caregiver she was going to call the others. She stepped out of the room and contacted them.

She stayed for a while, but then told me she was going home, but she'd be back. All the kids lived within a couple of blocks from me, Carole right around the corner. I was comforted knowing that all my children were so close.

She mentioned taking me outside when she returned. I knew I wouldn't be going outside, but I played along.

"Ok, hon. See you later," I said.

I know she would have stayed longer if she had thought that today was the day. But I also know she probably didn't want to be alone with me if it was. I wanted to make every effort to wait for each child to visit me before I would depart. That much I knew. Even if they couldn't all be there together, I would make sure each of them knew how much they meant to me. A strange feeling of peace came over me. One I hadn't experienced before.

The boys came by later that day. We made small talk, and I could see it in their faces, and hear it in their voices they were concerned. There wasn't much that could be done. My old heart was giving up. It had served me well for the past eighty-six years. I couldn't complain. I'd lived a good, long life.

It happened so quickly. One minute I was sitting on the couch trying to visit with them and the next thing I knew my two sons had carried me to bed.

I could hear voices. I had my eyes closed, but I could hear them clearly talking about me and what was about to happen. Peter called Carole and told her to get over here, and quickly. I was focusing on letting go, and not feeling any pain, but I'd wait for Carole.

I didn't want them to witness my dying, but that's the way this was going to go down. I had no choice. My only prayer was for me to go peacefully. God promised me that much.

"Mom, it's Carole. I'm here. It's ok. You can go be with Dad now. I love you." I clearly heard.

"Mom, I love you." I heard Peter say.

"Mom, you're free to go. We love you and don't want you to be in any more pain," Charles Jr. choked out.

But then the last thing I heard before I went was how much Carole would miss me and all the time we'd spent together. She said she'd always cherish the last ten years she lived nearby and wished it had been more. I couldn't tell her, but it had been more than enough. Her time with me was indeed special, and it was her love and patience, along with all the children that kept me going as long as I did.

And then, I was free. Free of pain, free of guilt and soaring high with the angels. I knew I was happy, so I was hoping there'd be a smile on my face. I was going to join Charles in Heaven, and I was going to set my children free. Free from being a caretaker, free of worry, and free to live their life as their father and I had so dearly wanted.

They'd given their love and time to me, and I would never be able to thank or compensate them enough. But rumor has it, they'd do it all over again, and not one of them would complain.

A Word from the Author

Eldercare is on the rise in the United States. It is not just with duty, but with love for our elderly that we should make sure their needs are taken care of. Other countries do it unselfishly, and we should too. When I visited my mother at the assisted living community which is walking distance from my home, I was saddened to learn that many older citizens never received visitors.

And although mom insisted she not give up her independence by keeping her apartment, she required 24 hour care toward the end of her life, but not a single day went by that she didn't receive a visit from me or my brothers, or our extended family, and she always got a phone call daily from us.

I realize in today's ever-changing society, many children are not living near their parent's and therefore daily contact is not possible. Making sure our elderly is taken care of by ensuring their residences are safe and the people who are interacting with them daily can be a viable solution.

Vote for legislation to keep our elderly safe and make housing affordable. These are all steps you can take to help the aging population. One day we'll all be in that category

Being there for mom was one of the most meaningful things I've done and I know she appreciated it so much.

Make sure you tell the people in your life how special they are. It will help you heal when the time comes.

A USA Today bestselling author, Debbie writes sweet contemporary romance and women's fiction. She lives in South Carolina with her husband and two dachshund rescues, Dash and Briar. She loves to hike, work in the garden, and on most sunny days, you can find her enjoying her backyard. She's an avid supporter of animal rescue, and as such, pledges to happily donate a percentage of all book sales to local and national rescue organizations. When you purchase any of her books, you're also helping animals.

To find out more about Debbie, check out her website at https://www.authordebbiewhite.com

Perfect Pitch

Ties That Bind

Passport To Happiness

The Missing Ingredient

The Salty Dog

The Pet Palace

Billionaire Auction

Billionaire's Dilemma

Coaching the Sub

Christmas Romance – Short Stories